International Praise for Jón Gnarr

"Jón Gnarr is a great man who I believe has helped change our opinion of politicians. By doing it his way he has shown that it is possible to not only channel the will of the people but also to influence it positively. With him governmental policies were formed for the people and by the people. I am very happy to give this award to the outstanding force that is Jón Gnarr."
—YOKO ONO, *on awarding Gnarr the Lennon-Ono Grant for Peace in 2014*

"Jón Gnarr has given the mayor profession a new human earnesty with radical stand-up style, and has chiseled away the stagnancy in that post with explosive humor."
—BJÖRK

"I love the mayor of Iceland."
—LADY GAGA

"Certainly my favorite mayor. No competition, in fact."
—NOAM CHOMSKY

"His gonzo approach to campaigning and governing made him world famous."
—GAWKER

"Boundlessly creative and extremely compas
—VICE

An original and creative individual."
—POPMATTERS

Gnarr's new memoir shares his incredible story and just might inspire more people to get involved in local politics."
—USA TODAY *on Gnarr*

Praise for The Indian

"It will not come as a surprise for anyone familiar with Jón's work that the narrative is often very funny, but...it is far from a purely comedic novel—really it is deeply tragic...The depiction of the isolation and pain experienced by Jón Gnarr is undoubtedly the greatest strength of this narrative. However, this is not the main issue here, but rather the way in which the author succeeds in describing the confusing existence of a child who does not understand his situation or why he feels the way he does."
— ÞORGERÐUR E. SIGURÐARDÓTTIR, BOKMENNTIR.IS *on* The Indian

THE INDIAN

—

Jón Gnarr

TRANSLATED FROM THE ICELANDIC BY
LYTTON SMITH

DEEP VELLUM PUBLISHING
DALLAS, TEXAS

Deep Vellum Publishing
2919 Commerce St. #159, Dallas, Texas 75226
deepvellum.org · @deepvellum

ISBN: 978-1-941920-12-1 (paperback) · 978-1-941920-13-8 (ebook)
LIBRARY OF CONGRESS CONTROL NUMBER: 2015930300

—

This book has been translated with financial support from:

 MIÐSTÖÐ ÍSLENSKRA BÓKMENNTA
ICELANDIC LITERATURE CENTER

—

Cover design & typesetting by Anna Zylicz · annazylicz.com

Text set in Bembo and Letter Gothic.
Bembo is a typeface modeled on typefaces cut by Francesco Griffo
for Aldo Manuzio's printing of *De Aetna* in 1495 in Venice. Letter Gothic was originally
designed by Roger Roberson for IBM sometime between 1956 and 1962.

Deep Vellum titles are published under the fiscal sponsorship of
The Writer's Garret, a nationally recognized nonprofit literary arts organization.

Distributed by Consortium Book Sales & Distribution.

Printed in the United States of America on acid-free paper.

○ ■ ◹ ✗ ◸ ■ ● ⊙ ◗ △ ✗

AUTHOR'S NOTE

A lot of people will undoubtedly wonder whether this is a biography or a novel. It's both. It isn't totally true, although there aren't any total lies in it either. I don't believe in lies. In fact I think lies are the greatest obstacle on our path towards spiritual development. But I shift quite a few things around. I write from memory. There are some things I have absolutely no recollection of myself, so I've had to rely on other people's memories. But all memory is fiction. Our brain is the greatest master of deceit in the universe.

A NOTE ON ICELANDIC ORTHOGRAPHY

The Icelandic alphabet is largely based on the Latin alphabet (as is English) but it includes ten extra letters, some of which derive from the runic tradition.

In addition to accented letters such as ó, í, and ý Icelandic also includes the letters ð and þ, known as "eth" and "thorn" respectively. They have slightly different pronunciations: ð, which comes between d and e in the Icelandic alphabet, is pronounced like the "th" in the English "that"; þ, which comes after y and ý, the antepenultimate letter of the alphabet, is pronounced like the "th" in English "thing." (The former, ð, is known as a "voiced fricative" whereas the latter, þ, is an "unvoiced fricative.")

The Icelandic alphabet has 32 letters: only six more in total than English, due to the fact that it lacks some English-language letters, including c and w.

I thought about all these names—
not once, not twice, not even
three times. I thought about them
no more. They thought themselves
into me, autocratic, ceaseless,
an automatic mantra wiping everything else away, clean gone from
my consciousness.

—

Þórbergur Þórðarson
On the Shore of Death's Ocean.
Unpublished.

X

In the beginning God created the heaven and the earth. And the earth was without form, and void; and darkness was upon the face of the deep. And the Spirit of God moved upon the face of the waters.

And God said:

"Let there be light!"

And there was light.

That was right around midday, January 2nd, 1967. At that very moment, I came into being. Before then, there was nothing; I was merely a shapeless form in the universe's consciousness, sleeping water, in water which wasn't yet water in an eternity where time doesn't exist.

At first, you don't know anything about your head. It's like someone has come up without warning and tagged you, and you're It. You're disoriented, confused. You don't know quite what to do. But, over time, little by little, you come to see things in context. Murmuring becomes speech and words. Everything gradually clarifies, taking on a fantastic light. You get on intimate terms with your existence. You gain experience. You come to discover the existence of others. Everything you do modifies your experience. And each experience is its own glorious discovery. The brain remembers things, reaches conclusions, and comes supplied with fluid for logical continuation, appropriate to the conditions. The past begins to accumulate like unsorted junk mail. She follows in your wake, wherever you go. You bear her on your back like a black garbage bag. She is your guide to the future, your tools for the tasks that await you. Over time, as the past grows, the more glimpses into the future she has. Before you know it, the past and the future begin to fight for your affections. You stop being amazed about the miracle, the fine craft, of your existence. Everything becomes familiar.

Eventually, the fantastic loses its magic, becomes merely a sequence of everyday incidents. But deep within, lodged between past and future, is The Now, the place from which you came before everything began. The Now is like coffee. You finish it and find, sitting there, the grounds.

Also, you discover it's best drunk hot.

△

My arrival was a total shock for my family. My mom was forty-five years old when she had me. Dad was fifty.

They knew they were too old to have a baby. Such a thing was out of the ordinary back then. Mom felt ashamed. She didn't try to hide her belly but she wasn't exactly waving a flag, either. It wasn't planned. I was on my way thanks to the carelessness of a feverish May moment at Hotel Flókalundur at Barðaströnd. I was christened Jón Gunnar. Jón in honor of Grandfather, Gunnar in honor of Aunt Gunna.

The due date was New Year's Day. Many people assumed that I'd be the first baby born that year, that there would be a picture of Mom and me in the paper. Mom flatly discounted the possibility. She didn't want any unnecessary attention. She's always kept to herself.

The doctors told her that, because of how old she was, it was very likely I'd be a retard. She was advised to have an amniocentesis to check for chromosomal defects. It was a fairly risky procedure; there was a risk of termination. Mom didn't want one. She didn't trust doctors; instead, she took the hand she'd been dealt without complaining or making a fuss. She'd learned from bitter experience to resign herself to her fate; she'd learned to accept the consequences of her actions. Mom won't tolerate dishonesty or excuses. Also, she'd learned that the easy, comfortable route is seldom the right route. Because she had gotten herself pregnant, she resolved to shoulder the responsibility for it, to nourish the child and raise it, retard or no.

My birth itself: another blow for the family. I'm obviously not retarded. A relief. But after the birth, another scary fact reveals itself: I'm a redhead. It couldn't have been more of a shock if I'd been born black.

Dad has dark hair. Mom has light hair. All my siblings have dark hair. There's no one with red hair in the family. Not a one. Not for a long way back in the line.

Grandma Anna immediately suspected some kind of hijinks. She'd always borne a grudge against red-haired folk. Redheads were, in her opinion, Northern gypsies, inferior to other people, useless except as shark-bait. She'd never known an honest redhead. Redheaded folk were vagabonds; they had thievish demeanors.

This led to much debate and some gossip. People doubted my paternity.

- Alas, I think there's not a bit of the boy I can call my own, joked Dad.

Grandma was not in the mood for laughter.

- I think you need to be home more often!

Grandma Anna never came to terms with it and never really took to me. In her eyes, I was a bastard, the black sheep of an otherwise magnificent herd, an ugly stain on the family tree. When someone praised or admired me, she readily muttered:

- Yes, he's intelligent and he's handsome, it can't be denied…but he's a redhead.

X

The new house is ready and we've moved in. It's big and smells wetly of fresh concrete.

I put my nose right up to the unpainted walls and huff the weird smell. The smell becomes a memory, fixed in my thoughts. Forty years later, I can still remember the smell; I relive the emotions each time I enter a new building. Cement, sand, and water. The scent of concrete.

Instead of window glass, there's plastic. Throughout the house, doors are missing. Outside, all around, there's a big mess: ditches and gravel and half-risen houses. Some houses are ready and people move in. Others are empty, surrounded by scaffolding. In between the houses are foundations waiting patiently for their own houses. Some of the foundations are hollow, only deep holes in the earth, with a puddle of water inside, like after a bombing raid. Over others a sheet has been poured. Dark iron reinforcements rise from the sheet. Scattered around are cement mixers and work-sheds. Large trucks drive back and forth in the runny mud. They're red and grey in color and fat in front and they're called Scania-Vabis. Beside each house there are concrete paths so people don't step in the slop surrounding everything.

Our house is a concrete, two-story townhouse, the last house in a block of three; our house is number one. In front of the house is a parking space. In the basement is a two-bedroom apartment with its own entrance, which faces out into the back garden. Mom and Dad rent it out.

Our apartment is huge. The entrance leads into a large hall. On the right hand there's a little storage room and a large kitchen overlooking the street. Straight ahead is a massive living room. Off from the living room is a television room with bookshelves. From the living room you can walk into a large storage room with a fridge. From the storage room, steps go down to the lower level where there's another storage closet. You can walk out to a balcony from the living room; the balcony faces south. From it, there are views over Fossvogsdalur and up as far as Kópavogur. The balcony has two doors: one into the living room, the other into the master bedroom.

When you go left from the hall, you pass a huge walk-in closet. Off the hall, on the left-hand side, two bedrooms face the street. The first is my sister Runa's room. Later, after she moves out, it becomes a telephone room. For a time, it's also Grandma Guðrún's bedroom. She lives with us while she waits for space to open up in the nursing home. Next to that room, in the corner, is Grandma Anna's room. She only lives with us for a few years, up until her death. After that, her room automatically becomes my room.

Next to my room there's a big bathroom with a bathtub and a little laundry nook for a washing machine and a sink. There's no window in the bathroom except for this weird roof-window which passes through the attic.

Beside the bathroom, at the end of the corridor, is a double bedroom. That's the largest bedroom; it has built-in closets. I sleep there for my first few years, along with Mom and Dad. And over the whole house there's unused storage space. The house is surrounded by a fenced-in lawn.

I have three siblings. They're all much older than me. My brother

Ómar is 25 years old when I'm born, and has long since left home. I have two sisters. Kristín is 20 years old and she's moved to Norway. Runa is 12 years older than me.

My family are ordinary, Icelandic people. As well as being a housewife, my mom is a female domestic: she works in the kitchen at City Hospital. She was born and grew up in Reykjavík, the youngest of eight sisters. My grandfather studied as a mason but didn't work much because he was sick. He had arthritis and died long before I was born. Mom told me about him. His fingers were so afflicted that he couldn't move them. Grandma Anna, Mom's mom, was a housewife. Despite being sick, my grandfather saw to it that my mom and her siblings were supported so that no one went without. They all lived together in a tiny apartment in the old part of Reykjavík. My mom's older brothers begged work here and there and foraged food for the family, usually fish which they bought from some men in the apartment below who owned a small motorboat. It was a tiny luxury.

My dad was born in 1918 during the Great Frost. That was a very difficult year for Icelanders, and for the whole world. In the same year, the Spanish flu raged; over 300 Icelanders died. But not Dad.

It was also the same year that Nicolai Bjarnason planted his sycamore garden on the corner of Suðurgata and Vonarstræti. He didn't know then that it would later become a parking lot.

My dad was born, and grew up, "out west," one of six siblings. His father was a foreman and a mailman. His mom was Grandma Guðrún.

I didn't ever meet my grandfather. He died long before I was born, like my other grandfather. He had tuberculosis and had to go to a sanatorium for several months. He recovered to full health, and went back west during the mild-tempered weather of the summer of 1954. He made the journey by boat across Breiðafjörður but sank on the way, somewhere in the middle of the fjord, together with all the men and all the rats. They never found debris or any sign of the boat. After that, Grandma moved south with the children.

Dad was over twenty when he came to Reykjavík. He wanted to be an actor and enrolled at a drama school but had to drop out because he was too poor. He couldn't afford to buy himself food, never mind pay the tuition. At that time, there was a need for policemen. Dad went along and, because he was unusually brave, he was hired on the spot. Reality won out over dreams.

He worked as a police officer for 40 years, a good employee who never missed a day of work. Despite this, he never gained any distinction in the force because of his political opinions: he was an affirmed Communist. He walked the streets, fought violent men, attended car crashes and took on things others didn't care to see. Finally, and as a formality, he was promoted to sergeant and got to sit in the lobby. By that time, he had really weak legs because of his decades walking around in inferior shoes on behalf of the State. Later, the State made up for its stinginess by giving him replacement hips.

Grandma Anna and sister Runa, who has just completed Confirmation move into the new house with me and my parents.

Runa isn't happy about the move since she's being torn away from her friends and having to move to the "ass-end of nowhere." Fossvogur is a suburb of Reykjavík which many consider the absolute limit of the habitable world. It's more or less the country, since sheep graze in the valley and even the town of Kópavogur is some place far off in the distance.

Grandma Anna has gotten senile. She doesn't always know who we are. She doesn't know who I am. At times she's also really angry about something or other. She always thinks that she's being abused in some way. She cries a lot and occasionally screams. She believes she never gets fed. She'll have only just finished a meal and gone into her bedroom when she comes back out again.

– I gather there's not going to be any food, just as usual.
She starts to sob.
– Aren't I allowed to have some food? she asks Mom.
– You just ate, says Mom.
At this, Grandma breaks down and bursts into tears.
– You should be ashamed of yourself, treating me like this, she wails.
Mom sighs.
– I was never so mean and stingy a mother that I scrimped on giving you enough to eat.

Any food she can find she stashes in her room. Sometimes she creeps out into the kitchen, taking food and bringing it back to her bedroom to hide. I swear I've seen her slip a whole fistful of fish fingers into her bathrobe pocket. In the drawer of her dresser, in with her underwear and her trinkets, lie remnants of moldy bread and putrefying meatballs. Mom regularly goes through her things; a bad smells gushes up, but Grandma screams and complains.

– Are you planning to starve me all the way to the grave?

Sometimes she give Runa her clothes. Then she cries because Runa doesn't want to go out in them.

– Mom, Grandma keeps giving me this hideous blouse.

She holds up a knitted northern shirt. Mom laughs.

– I can't stand it when she does this!

One time, Runa came into her bedroom to find Grandma setting folded underwear on her bed. Runa got really mad.

– Mom, will you take this disgusting stuff away?

Grandma cried her eyes out when she saw that Runa didn't want to wear her underwear. She thought she was ungrateful and snobbish.

– Shame on you, disdaining these good things I'm giving you!

– Mom!?!

Our cat, Steamball, also moves into the new house with us. Steamball is a really dangerous brute. She won't tolerate strangers and attacks people who come to visit us. She comes running and jumps on people without warning, lunging with her mouth and claws extended.

One time, a woman who worked with my Mom visited. Steamball was sunbathing in the windowsill. The woman went to stroke her but Mom warned against it, telling her that she was bad-tempered. The woman carried on regardless, leaning towards Steamball.

– What a pretty little kitt–

Steamball lashed out a paw and sliced up her cheek. Then she hissed and attacked her legs. Mom had to pry her off the woman and throw her into the bedroom.

In almost everyone's opinion, Steamball is mental. But she isn't insane enough to have ever attacked me. Even though I've treated her really badly ever since I was a baby. I'd pick her up by the scruff of her fur and carry her about like a purse, or drag her behind me by the tail. She never once clawed me or hissed at me. Not even when I dressed her in clothes or decorated her with scotch tape. At most, she tried to avoid me. And when I slept, she snuck up to me and coiled herself around my head. Perhaps she felt some mysterious solidarity with me. In the end, we couldn't have her any longer because she became even fouler-tempered with age. Dad took her outside somewhere and shot her with his service revolver.

●

I walk around the apartment and get to know it bit by bit: its dark crannies and its open spaces. I smell everything. The surroundings shift and change color; objects vanish and others come into existence. Bookshelves and odd cabinets spring up where before there were walls. Every day has a new smell.

One day when I wake up there are carpets in the room instead of the cold stone that was there before. New doors, too. New colors on the walls. A mirror that reflects everything except me. I am too little.

This is my world. It consists of me, Mom, Runa, and Grandma Anna. And sometimes Dad.

I go outside with Runa.

Suddenly everything around the house has become green. Grass. I don't know where it came from. Everything happens so fast.

All at once, I'm in the bath. Runa bathes me. She gives me something blue that is shaped like a stone but still soft. It's got a good smell.

– Take a bite.

– What is this?

– Candy.

I look at her. She nods her head, wearing an encouraging expression. I like candy. It's got a good smell and tastes good.

I bite gently on the thing. It burns my tongue. A disgusting taste fills my mouth and gums up my teeth. My lower lip scorches. I spit, trying to get rid of the bitter, stinging taste. Runa rolls about laughing.

- That's soap! What sort of moron eats soap?

I look at the stick of soap with my teeth marks in it. Runa washes my hair. Then she sprays cold water on my back with the hand shower; it makes me gasp for breath. She laughs peals of laughter because she finds it hilarious that it gives me such a shock.

Runa finds me annoying. She won't put up with me, and often gets upset when Mom orders her to look after me.

- I want to go out with the girls.

- Can't they come round?

- Oh, get real!

I'm not allowed to go into her bedroom. If I touch something or damage it she says she will kill me. But I still like being around her.

[…] then there is Runa, who was born in '55;
she has completed her high school education and
works as an office girl. It is the case that he
gets on well good with Runa if they are alone,
but if people come to visit Runa then he won't
stop needling her; he keeps opening the door to
her bedroom, and says exceedingly annoying things.
These types of incidents have happened many times,
and Runa has from time to time tried to stop him
and see that he leaves her and her guests in
peace. The parents feel that the boy looks up to
Runa, and the mother says that the girl ought
to facilitate that more, to let him play, instead
of separating herself from him—even though she
herself has at times had to seek help when he
has been at his most difficult: making mischief
and acting out and using bad language.

(National Hospital, Psychiatric Ward,
Children's Hospital Trust, 08/02/1972)

■

Then all at once everything stops changing. One day everything's found its place and is there forever. It's like we've always lived here. The past blurs, dissipates, and vanishes.

We subscribe to two newspapers: *The Morning News* and *The Nation's Will*. *The Nation's Will* is a Communist paper. The delivery boy isn't allowed to put it through the mail slot because if Grandma Anna sees it she begins to cry.

– Am I to understand that you continue reading this muck?

Then she rips the paper into pieces and throws it in the bin.

Dad reads *The Nation's Will*. He finds it both more remarkable and more enjoyable a newspaper than what he calls *The Mug's News*.

One day, Grandma Anna stops crying and complaining. She goes to the hospital and dies. Her bedroom empties, and all at once her bed becomes my bed. My toys have been moved into her room and are now inside a big storage closet. My bedroom becomes my world. In a single night, Runa's bedroom has transformed into a telephone room. Runa has gone, too. I don't know where. There's no one left but me and Mom, and sometimes Dad.

Mom dresses me in my rain gear and sends me outside.

- Don't go far.

I'm not going anywhere. I think it's fun to play in the mud outside the house. I make a road and drive my car along it.

While I play, my surroundings transform from unbuilt to built. Huge machines come and go; some strangers call by. Sometimes, these callers talk to me. They are entertaining and have turned-up sleeves.

Then the mud disappears, and I'm sitting on asphalt.

✕

Home life is terribly silent. When I wake up, Dad's gone to work. He eats his pickled meat and porridge for breakfast. I eat Cheerios.

Dad doesn't come back home until late in the evening. He watches the news and falls asleep. Sometimes he talks to me in the evenings, when he's about to take his nap.

I love chatting with Dad. He knows so much and there's so much I want to know. We watch *The Latest,* which is about new science and technology, and he explains to me what I don't understand.

Mom doesn't know anything. She doesn't care. She doesn't want to know how planes can fly and why ships don't sink even though they're overweight.

– I don't know, she says, sadly.

– But don't you want to know?

– Not if I don't need to know.

She talks to me in short, direct sentences. When Dad isn't home I ask her the things I don't understand.

– I don't know, ask your Dad, is her answer.

But Dad is usually very tired when he's done working. He works all day and sometimes at night. Sometimes he has to work on Christmas. He just comes home to eat then goes back out to work.

When Dad is that tired, it's like he doesn't hear me even though I'm right in front of him.

– What's quicksilver, Dad?

- Yes, he replies, looking at a spot in the air.

- Anton says that quicksilver is a stone that's like water.

- Well, that's good.

Dad's odd. He is often distracted.

Gummi once asked me whether he's deaf. He was outside in his garden with his dad when Dad walked past. Gummi's dad said hello but Dad didn't respond. He raised his voice and said hello again but Dad still didn't answer.

He isn't deaf. Mom took him to have a hearing test. Dad is not deaf. He's just a bit distracted.

Dad also often confuses people. Sometimes when he's reading the paper, he's convinced one of his friends has died.

- Kristján's dead, he says suddenly.

- Kristján who? asks Mom.

- Kristján Einarsson, my friend.

Then Mom shakes her head and rolls her eyes, goes over to him, and looks at the paper.

- That's not Kristján!

- It says so right here.

- That's another Kristján. That's not your cousin Kristján.

- Isn't it? Are you totally sure?

- Yes, I am totally sure.

- How can you tell?

Mom gets irritated.

- Just by looking at the picture. It's not him.

- Well, says Dad and smoothes the paper as though he's sorry his cousin isn't dead.

He never remembers anyone's name. Sometimes he calls my friends names they aren't called. I have three friends. They're called Gummi, Stebbi, and Anton and they all live on the same street as me. Dad's met them many times. He thinks they're all called Siggi. I don't have any friends called Siggi. I don't know why he thinks I have a friend named Siggi. Maybe he had a friend, when he was a boy, called Siggi. Perhaps he thinks all little boys are called Siggi.

My father is a Communist. Mom votes for the Independence Party. My dad is opposed to the Independence Party. He calls them conservatives or, sometimes, the damn conservatives. Conservatives are the enemies of Communists. A conservative publishes *The Morning News*.

Mom doesn't have the same interest in politics as Dad. She doesn't care that they're enemies. She simply opts for the Independence Party because her mother and father did, and so do all her family. She thinks traditions and customs are important.

When Mom has made a decision, she very rarely changes her mind, and doesn't ever feel like talking about it. She has no interest in innovation and ideas. She's happy when things are as they always have been. If everything is OK, in her opinion, and things work, there's no need to change anything; ideas and speculation and that sort of thing are an unnecessary waste of time. But Mom likes people. She tells stories about them and likes to wonder what they're up to. Though she's not a gossip.

Mom has strong views about people too. Some are good and others are not. She is not snobbish and does not pick favorites by class or status. But she has her opinions about people she doesn't know or doesn't have information about from a reliable source. She also judges people based on her personal experience of them. And when she's judged someone, that becomes her opinion of them. If Mom doesn't like someone, there's little chance it will change. If she clashes with someone, she stops talking to them.

Sometimes when I get into an argument at school, I try to talk to my Mom.

- He's so irritating.

- Then stop talking to him.

- What do you mean?

- Just never talk to him again.

- What if he talks to me?

- If he tries to talk to you, you should walk past him. Leave like you haven't seen him.

Mom doesn't complicate things for herself. She doesn't mind that Dad's a Communist. It's all the same to her. He occasionally makes feeble attempts to draw her into political debates, on some specific issues, but always without success.

- It's the conservatives who support this war, they're the ones who dragged us into it—against the will of the majority of the population.

- I don't know anything about war.

- You vote conservative, though.

- Yes, sure.

- Isn't it your personal responsibility, then, to inform yourself about what you're voting for?

- I don't see that it matters either way.

- Doesn't matter?!? How can you say that?

- I don't care a bit. I just say what I want.

- You don't care who runs the country or how they do it?

- Absolutely.

- But when these same people jeopardize our security, don't you think it's time to make a decision, time for each and every voter in the country to reflect on the consequences of their voting?

– I don't know anything about that.

– Why don't you study it, then?

– Because I'm not interested in it, Kristinn!

– You're not interested in it?!

– No.

– And you think that's logical?

– Enough! Stop bugging me. I'm tired of this stupid debate.

– So that's the end of it?

– Yes, I do what I want and I vote how I want and I don't have to explain it to you or anyone else!

Mom reads Danish newspapers. She occasionally gets a pile of them from her friends.

I think the news in them is boring. It's nothing but recipes and interviews with princesses and people who are famous in Denmark. All the images are of women in ridiculous fashion get-up.

I read *Youth*. That's a cool paper, especially because of its comic strips. Mom gets it for me, and sometimes she also gets *Duck Tales*. I think Donald Duck is great. He's my favorite character. He's like me. He has great ideas that usually fail. Donald is a good person but keeps making inadvertent mistakes. That's me, too. He's always working for Uncle Scrooge but he still always owes people money. Scrooge is miserly but he's alright because he's loaded and often invites Donald and Huey, Dewey, and Louie to accompany him on exhilarating adventures, to countries that perhaps no one else has ever gone to, even far out into space. I also like The Beagle Boys. They're always trying to steal money from Scrooge. I'm confident that I'll be like Donald Duck when I grow up.

Mickey Mouse strikes me as an annoying guy. I don't understand people who think he's funny. I always flick past him. He doesn't even live in Duckburg and he's always messing with things that aren't his business. All he ever does is walk his dog; he never has any good ideas. But his friend Goofy is okay, especially when he eats nuts and turns into Super Goof. And also Dr. Einmug. He's a scientist and he invented a time machine.

Most of the others I think are dull. The old grandmother in the countryside and Clarabelle Cow, for example, are boring old biddies.

Daisy Duck is the most boring of all. She's conceited, a bile-inducing girlfriend who's always angry at poor Donald though he's always trying to be kind to her. And you never really know if she's his girlfriend or not. What is she always up to with Gladstone Gander, for example? I hope my wife won't be like that.

Dad also gets two magazines. One is the *Police Gazette*. It's really dull. It mainly contains articles about traffic matters and interviews with cops about boring things. All the pictures are of cops celebrating birthdays or winning sports prizes, usually for swimming.

The other newspaper is called *News from the Soviet Union*. I read it, sometimes. I don't understand it, though. It's full of weird news: NEW TRACTORS FOR NIZHNEVARTOVSK! Accompanying the story is a picture of a train full of tractors and happy people waving flags. Nizhnevartovsk. I've no idea where it is. I can't even say it. Niss-knee-wart-off-sk! It's in the Soviet Union. That's the country the Communists call home.

The people in the paper are always cheerful and always have flags. Sometimes there are also pictures of soldiers on parade in the city center. It's like it's always June 17 in the Soviet Union, Independence Day. Anton says that the Soviet Union is a horrible country and all the pictures there are fake. He says that if a person isn't happy and doesn't have a flag then the secret police come and arrest and torture them, and that lots of people get sent to labor camps in Siberia where it's very cold, always winter and never summer.

Anton knows an awful lot. But he doesn't know everything. For example, he told me that girls don't have pricks.

– Then how do they pee? I asked.

He thought for a while, then shrugged his shoulders.

– Out their ass, I guess.

I found this weird. I was too scared to ask my mom. Moms don't like to talk about things like that. And I never thought to ask my dad. Some things you just can't talk about.

There are two girls who live in our street and who aren't annoying. I asked one of them when she was outside skipping.

– How do girls pee?

She looked at me like I was the stupidest boy in all the world.

– Anton says that girls pee out their butts, I added.

– Tony Terylene? she asked, making a face as though he's a dubious source of information.

– Yes.

– Girls don't pee out their butts. Are you being a stupid jerk?

– Then how do girls pee?

– They pee out their pee-holes.

I went directly to Anton with this new information. As soon as he came to the door, I whispered:

– They pee out their pee-holes.

- Pee-holes?

- Yes, I said, with the air of one who knows everything.

Mostly, I was glad to finally know something he didn't know.

- What's a pee-hole?

I didn't know. I ran back, but the girl was gone.

Sometimes Dad gets sent pictures of men. They're large, thick-framed pictures. The men always look pissed; they wear black clothing, and often have a black hat. They're really old. I know that some of the men are officers in the Soviet Union. Sometimes there are pictures of them in the papers, usually standing on a balcony and waving to a crowd of people with flags. The men are the complete opposite of the people. The people are super happy, but the men don't smile. I don't understand how that's possible. Why are the men always so serious? Why aren't they as happy as the people with flags? And why are there always soldiers and tanks in the center of the towns?

When the pictures come, it starts an argument between my parents. Dad wants to hang the pictures up in the living room along with the family photos. Mom puts her foot down.

- Why not?

- Because it is totally out of the question!

- I can't put up a picture I've been given?

- No.

- Can I hang it in the television room?

- Not a chance.

- Why not?

- Because it's absurd.

- Absurd? What's absurd about it?

- If you can't see it yourself then I won't discuss it with you.

- It's a gift for me.

- Enough of this damn prattle! You're not hanging this picture; we're done talking about it.

Mom always has the last word. She's the decider. And since my dad doesn't get to hang the pictures up in the living room, he hangs them up down in the basement. Hanging there are the comrades Gromyko, Brezhnev, Khrushchev, and Stalin, watching each other with their grave expressions.

There's a horrible man in the living room. He's wearing bright red clothes and has a long, white beard. I try to clamber up my Dad's leg. He just laughs and turns me back to face the man. He looks at me, says something and stretches out his hands. He tries to take me. I get scared and start crying. Mom comes and picks me up. She walks me over to the man. He holds his hat towards me in one hand. I scream in terror, smear myself against Mom, and bury my face in her shoulder.

We're in the living room. I'm not allowed to get into the Christmas presents. I'm not to play with any of the Christmas stuff. It's for decoration. It's dangerous. My dad is wearing his police uniform. He gives me a present. There's another cop with him. They're happy.

– This is for you, he says, in a friendly manner.

He has a gentle expression. I've already got the present. I'm allowed to open it.

In the package is a red truck. It's mine. There are barrels on the truck bed.

When I'm playing, Mom comes over with other packages and gives them to me. I don't want them.

– I'm ready to go out, I say.

– You can have this, too.

I don't want it.

– I am ready to go out.

Mom smiles. She smiles beautifully.

She dresses me in my raingear.

- Shall we go to Róló? she asked.

I nod. Róló is a place with playground equipment and a fence around it. There are swings and a seesaw and a giant sandbox with iron hollows that you can sit in and shovel with. There are kids there to play with.

I have on red rain pants and a blue rain jacket. Mom also puts me in black boots, hat, and gloves. Then we walk to the playground.

It's always raining at Róló. Mom often takes me there and leaves me. I have everything I need there. I own the swings and seesaw. I also own the hut. The other kids can play on them, sure, but only if they ask for permission. If someone tries to play without asking for permission then I pull his hair and he begins to cry.

I also own one of the boys at the playground. He is called Ragnar. He doesn't need to ask for permission because I own him.

Once time, Ragnar and I ran away from the playground. We set car tires up against the fence and climbed over when the women weren't looking. We ran away. We got lost. There were lots of cars. First Ragnar started crying and then I did. Then I closed my eyes and lay down. We've never done it again.

Sometimes I go over to where the women are. They sit and smoke. They wipe my nose and give me sugar cubes.

My sister Runa comes to fetch me. My mittens have got wet. They have a strange smell when they get wet; you can drink water from them by sucking them. She undresses me out of my rain pants and boots. The boots are stuck to the rain pants with elastic. She holds them and makes them walk. That's funny.

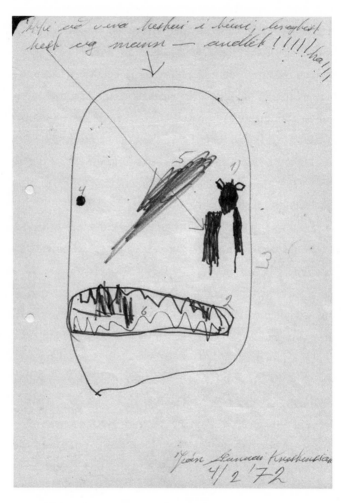

Drawn by Jón in the hospital at age 5 on 02/04/1972,
with notes from the doctor: "Was supposed to be
a horse in a meadow, changed into a horse and a
man—face!!!! what!!!"

▲

[…] This nearly 3-year-old boy was admitted
because of *hernia inguinalis*; it had lasted for
the past 2 months. He has always been plucky
but also extremely rowdy, perhaps as a result
of a hyperkinetic disorder; he is never calm
around objects, but gets agitated and rages
at everything.

(St. Joseph's Hospital,
Landakoti, 10/02/1969)

■

…In the summer of 1969, Jón Gunnar was in
preschool; he was considered unruly and rowdy
but not especially problematic; he truly enjoyed
school. This was, however, only for the summer.
In the fall of 1970, he was a kindergartener
in a little residential area, but the women
employed there gave up on him. He did everything
"madly."

(National Hospital, Psychiatric Ward,
Children's Hospital Trust, 02/04/1972)

X

I give my mother the slip. She calls and I don't answer. She's annoying and I don't want to be around her. I run as fast as I can. I'm going to hide so I look for a hiding place. Mom calls for me again. But there's nowhere to hide, just big streets and cars.

I run out into the road. A large car honks at me and I startle. I didn't notice it. It just came out of nowhere. I jump onto a traffic island. Cars rush past on either side of me. I can't run back across the street. The cars come towards and away from me no matter which way I turn. I'm stuck. I'm afraid, too.

The whole time I'm looking this way and that. Cars hurtle past at tremendous speeds, making deafening sounds. I'm never ever going to get out of here. Mom won't be able to reach me. I burst into tears. Nobody does anything. Cars don't care about boys like me. Instead of stopping, they just increase their speed and make more noise. My head is spinning. I shut my eyes and let myself fall to the grass. Grass has a good smell. Yet I can also smell something oily. Far away, I hear my mother calling.

- Lie down right there and don't move!

I sink slowly and calmly into the grass, into the soil, deep down into the earth, towards the worms. I hum and the sounds around me fall silent.

Someone takes my shoulder. A man.

- Are you alright, little fella?

I don't say anything. I won't say anything. I want to be left alone to recover. I'm scared.

But the man is tough. He lifts me up and takes me in his arms. I feel okay with him. I am safe, secure. He walks across the street with me. The cars are afraid of him and slow down. He owns all the cars and is in charge of them.

Across the street, Mom is waiting. She's different than usual. She isn't tired; instead, she seems upset and she has tears in her eyes. It reassures me to see that.

– God, Jesus, child!

[…] The mother is often tired; she is stout, neatly dressed, pleasant in appearance, has a pessimistic outlook, finds it a little hard to express herself, yet has a fairly good insight into the boy's difficulties and the extent to which he differs from his peers […] it is clear that the mother finds it too much dealing with her challenging son […] the parents, especially the mother, seems to truly realize the boy has problems so have sought assistance here; both seem well-motivated, though mainly the mother.

(National Hospital, Psychiatric Ward, Children's Hospital Trust, 02/04/72)

I'm in my best clothes. Mom dressed me in them. I'm wearing my jacket, too. We're sitting in a waiting room. I'm reading my newspaper. The smell is overwhelming, deep and alien, sweet and clean. I don't know what makes a smell like this. Maybe a swimming pool?

- Jón, it's your turn, says a woman.

Mom indicates I should go. I stand up and pad down the hall but find no one there. Only the smell. I walk back and go into another corridor.

I try to open a door but it's locked. I look around me and see that the doctor is following me. He doesn't say anything. I don't say anything either; I simply walk in and sit in a chair. He closes the door and sits opposite me.

I sink back into my newspaper. It's a cowboys-and-Indians comic. I don't know how to read it but I look at the pictures. I look at them really well. The Indians are spying on the cowboys. Indians are good and cowboys are evil.

- Don't you want to take off your jacket? he asks.

I am hot. I take off my jacket without looking up from the paper and throw it on the floor.

The doctor is called Einar. He's fun but weird. Whenever I say something he thinks about it and writes in his book. I don't know what he is writing. Maybe he's writing a story. Maybe it's a story about a boy like me who disobeys his mother. Maybe he understands me; maybe he understands that I'm not bad. But maybe I am bad.

Sometimes I pull other kids' hair and I'm mean to Mom. Sometimes I damage my toys when I'm playing with them. Sometimes people are angry at me and scold me, but I usually don't know why. There are bad guys who come and take rude boys.

There's a crane up on the shelf.

– What's that? I ask, and point to the crane.

– It's a crane.

– It's strange.

– It is made from Bilofix.

I look at the crane. Bilofix is a toy like Lego. It has pieces of wood with holes and colorful plastic screws that fix them together. There are also tires. I've played with Bilofix before.

– I want it, I say.

He stands up, fetches the crane, and gives it to me. It's really cool. It has a band in it that can be pulled up by turning a wheel. Some of the screws are loose. I undo them completely and put them in different places. I'm going to take the crane apart and put it back together again. Sometimes I build things from Lego bricks, like houses, then throw them against the floor so that they smash. It's okay to break Legos because you can always build it again. Bilofix is like that. Meccano too. Meccano's just the same, only made of iron.

The crane falls apart. I can't put it together again. The band has gotten all tangled. But it's okay. I haven't damaged anything. I know I haven't because Einar isn't angry. He just looks curiously at me then writes in his book.

I wind the band around the sticks and throw it all on the floor. Then I pick up the paper that comes with Bilofix. It's got instructions and pictures but it's all too difficult.

- I don't get it.

Einar stands up, takes the Bilofix, and puts it in a box. Then he sits back down, and writes in the book.

- Your mother tells me you don't enjoy playing with other kids?

It's true. I don't think it's any fun. I think it's better to be by yourself. I never know what they want. They take toys and they confuse everything. I can't tell from their expressions what they are thinking. They're just weird.

Often I get bewildered when I'm around them and that makes me feel bad. Sometimes, I feel so bad that I start crying. I'm afraid of them. Still, they don't do anything nasty to me. I just don't understand them and they don't understand me. It's like we don't talk the same language. They're smarter than me. They know all kinds of things I don't know. And no one ever tells them off. Though I'm stronger.

But they're always surprising me. I don't think they're annoying. I don't want to be bad around them. But when I get scared, I pull their hair. Ideally, I just want them to go away and leave me to be me.

- Why don't you want to play with them? he asks.

I don't know what to say.

- Are you being shy, Jón?

I'm not shy. But I am afraid. I'm afraid of people, including Einar. They don't understand me. I want him to stop talking to me and to stop looking at me. I want to go home and go into my bedroom. I don't want to be me. I don't want to be here. I want to go far inside myself, further, further, deep down where no one can bother me and no one is mad at me.

Sometimes, when I'm completely asleep, I feel strange. My thumb seems gigantic and I disappear inside it. Inside the thumb, two people are talking. They speak slowly and I can't hear what they are saying. They don't notice me. I walk past them and into a long hallway, down some steps and down a long stairway. I walk along another long hallway and at the end is a room that is as soft as a cotton ball. I come back outside myself and lie on the floor in the room. And I sleep.

– Jón?

Suddenly I hear a roaring from outside the house. The floor is shaking.

– What's going on? I ask.

– What do you think? he asks in return.

I do not know. Perhaps it's some battle we're fighting. Perhaps it's Satan. Maybe he's come to get me. Satan knows about me. He is the Bad Guy.

Once, Mom called me and told me to come into the telephone room. She handed me the phone and said a woman wanted to talk to me. I was scared. The woman asked if I was rude. I denied it, but she said she knew everything about me. She asked me if I knew what happens to bad boys. I didn't speak. She said that Satan comes to get the rude boys like me and stuffs them into a black bag. She asked if I wanted Satan to come get me. I said no.

After the call, I went into my room. I couldn't catch my breath and I was only able to fill my lungs by yawning. I was seriously tired and wanted to disappear into the giant thumb. Satan is an ugly name.

The sound keeps going. Einar switches between looking at me and writing in his book.

– It's just coming from the corner, I say.

I'm bad and ugly. Maybe Satan really has come to get me. Maybe he's coming up out of the ground. Maybe Einar is friends with Satan. Maybe Mom won't care if Satan takes me. Maybe she's already gone. I might never go back home. It's like a heavy slab is laying across my chest. I'm defenseless: I don't have my knife with me.

I jump to my feet and listen. The sound is coming from the radiator. Sometimes a sound comes from the radiator in my room. But that's a quiet buzz and not a great noise like this. Then I figure out what it is. It's just some drilling. I breathe easy. I sit back down.

– Were you frightened, Jón? Were you afraid of the sound?

– No.

– Do you know how old you are?

– Six.

– Which school do you go to?

– Foxvox!

– Fossvogs?

– That's what I said.

– Is school fun?

– Yes.

– Who is your teacher?

– Her name is Marta. I've got a schoolbag, too. It's red with a picture on the front, of a boy standing by a tree, giving a girl an apple.

– Is it a nice bag?

– Stebbi says that it's a girl's bag.

– Who is Stebbi?

– He's my friend.

– So you have friends?

I don't want to discuss these things. It's no fun. I like the way my bag smells. The scent of leather is my favorite smell. I love my bag because it's good to breathe inside it. Sometimes I'll stick my face in it and breathe the nice smell and then I feel good. Sometimes, it smells like whatever snacks were in my bag.

Smell is very important. My sister Runa sometimes teases me by making me smell baker's ammonia. That's bad. I think all smells are good, except others' poop and pee smells, and the smell of cucumbers.

The smell of cucumber is the worst smell in the world. It makes me sick. Once my mom tried to give me bread with slices of cucumber. She threw the slices away and put pâté in its place. But I could still smell it. The smell of cucumber is so strong. It's green and spiky.

There's paper on the table and whiteboard markers. Markers smell good. I like sniffing markers. When you sniff colored markers, you've got to be careful not to write on your nose. The red one smells of oranges.

I take a piece of paper and a marker and draw a picture of Satan with his bag. I also draw a knife and a gun to kill Satan with. If Satan comes, I'll kill him with a knife.

– Who's this? asks Einar, looking at the images.

– This is Satan.

– Who's that?

– He's just some guy.

– Do you know him?

– No.

– Do you know where he lives?

– He's friends with The Octopus.

– Who's that?

I don't want to talk about it. I get bored so I shut up. Maybe it will all go away if I don't talk about it. I'm not talking about Satan. I don't even think about it. And I'm not going to talk about Salarías, either.

Einar looks at me curiously. I wish he'd stop doing that. I don't want him to see me. Maybe he can see what I'm thinking. My mom can tell when I'm about to do something. Maybe he's thinking about what to do with really bad and ugly boys like me.

I get the toys out of the toy-box and put them on the table: a large bull, some miniature cowboys, a lion, and an elephant. The bull attacks the cowboys and kills them all. It also kills the lion and elephant and butts them off the table. I put the bull on the table and build a fort around it so no one can get to it to kill or hurt it. I take everything that's on the table and arrange it around the bull.

I take the desktop phone and make a fence with the cable. A dial tone sounds from the handset. That's okay. Nobody can hurt the bull. The bull can look after itself. It can butt anyone who tries to kill it. If Satan comes, the bull will gore him to death.

When the bull is completely safe, I go back to studying my comics.

Einar writes in his book. I read the paper. I recognize J. That's my initial. But it's difficult to draw. Though not as difficult as drawing R and S.

Stebbi knows how to read. Mom once pointed to the letters on the fridge and asked us what they spelled. I didn't know. There were so many characters. But Stebbi knew: A – D – M – I – R – A – L.

Einar goes out and calls Mom. They talk; I don't listen to them. I don't care what they're saying.

– Put your coat on, says Mom.

I get dressed while reading my paper.

I don't want to be there. I want to go away and to be left alone. All of a sudden we're outside. I won't ever go back again.

Jón Gunnar is my research subject on account of his lack of restraint and his isolation from other children [...] His expression suggests he is somewhat confused: "lost." He seems to barge headlong without taking account of what he is up to, and without seeming aware of his surroundings. Jón Gunnar sat with his mother in the waiting room, greeted me without looking at me and brought with him a comic he was reading. He was headed into the wrong corridor, but he got his bearings and then was on his way into another room in the right hallway before he made it to my room. He walked straight in, seemed to have no reaction to me as a stranger, sat at the desk and began reading his paper. He was wearing a winter coat; when he seemed to be starting to get quite warm, I suggested that he seemed like he might want to take off his jacket. He carried on doing what he was doing while he struggled out of the jacket and dropped it on the floor beside him.

After a little while in the room with me he began to look around; he saw something up on the bookcase and said "I want that." It was a crane made of Bilofix; he immediately began to tackle it; although the crane was fairly complicated, there was no hesitation from Jón Gunnar: he took it apart, loosening a screw here, another there, and tightening a nut in a third place. It took just half a minute until the crane got totally entangled; the band inside it slackened completely and the crane started to fall apart. Then Jón Gunnar took the band, wrapped it around the whole thing, and tried to tie the band. That failed, so he let it fall to the ground and began looking at the instructions for the Bilofix, which had many pictures. He said he couldn't do this, nor this, nor this; eventually, he found the easiest part, and said "I can do that." He made no effort to carry it out; he just left the Bilofix mess there on the floor, and didn't seem bothered by it, even though he had to walk over it when he wanted to play with something else.

When we went out into the corridor, he began to hear a thundering from outside the building. There were people drilling into the wall. The lad looked towards the window and asked what that was; I wanted him to tell me what he thought it was. "It's just from the corner," he said, and tried to let that solution suffice; when the noise increased, he began to look back in its direction and went towards it. Once he saw the radiator, he said, "It's just from the radiator." But we drew closer to the radiator, and he began to listen to it. Then he said, as if nothing were more self-explanatory, "It's just some-one drilling outside."

[…] When he started playing with small animals and

cowboys and such like on the table, he described to me what was happening. He selected the bull, which perpetrated the most awful bloodbath: it killed every single one of the animals and most of the people. When it was over, he took it up and made fences on the table around the bull. He used whatever was available: for example he took a phone and used that as part of his protective wall. He didn't see this as interfering in any way; however, the buzzing from the handset continued for about 5 min. Then he said, "I'm going to read my paper." He got onto his knees and read for about 10 minutes and was completely in his own world, unaware of what was taking place around him. He never once looked at me.

He drew a picture of his own accord and told me that it was Satan. I asked for more information about this person, and he said that he is friends with the octopus.

I cannot say for sure what I have discovered in my very limited contact with this child, based on the hour that I was with him. I think it would be safe to say that he never looked at me from beginning to end. He seemed to show absolutely no consideration for me. He went away and seemed no wiser than when he came.

(National Hospital, Psychiatric Ward,
Children's Hospital Trust, 07/03/1973)

I went out and got a few big rocks. I had to make several trips because they were so heavy. I gathered them in a pile by the porch. Then I snuck in with them, one by one, without my mom seeing. I was sure she'd ban them. I put some in my Liverpool FC bag and wrapped my coat around others; I took them up into my room and hid them in a closet.

When I was done carrying all the stones I went back out and gathered firewood. I filled my Liverpool bag with thin sticks and kindling. Then I took the stones out of the closet and arranged them in a circle on the floor. I put the sticks and the kindling in the middle of the ring.

I built my fireplace like the Indians in cowboy movies do. It would be cozy to lie in bed and read *Duck Tales* beside a crackling campfire. Mom would certainly be thrilled when she saw it. Dad would sit beside me, or maybe at the campfire, when he came home from work. We could go out to the Elliðaár River. I could catch a few salmon and we could come back and grill them over my fire.

I'm an Indian. I'm in a tribe of Indians. Mom won't sew me Indian clothes. She's stopped sewing because of the arthritis in her fingers. But I've got a knife and a headdress with feathers in it, which I bought in a toy store in the Grímsbær shopping center. It's really very handsome, with a brown plastic stretchy headband that goes around your forehead. The plastic piece goes over your ears and hangs down from them.

On the headpiece there's all sorts of patterns; colorful feathers stick up into the air from your forehead and hang down over your shoulders. These feathers are like the ones chieftains have.

The knife is real, big and strong, in a leather holster that has a glorious leather smell. Dad calls him Sting. But it's an Indian knife, a real and authentic Indian knife: Made in U.S.A. I do not know what that means but I think it is some kind of Indian mark. Maybe it's the name of some Indian chief. A knife is the only thing an Indian needs. Everything else can be taken away from him. He can be in everyday clothes and he can look like everyone else. But he never forgets his knife. He needs it in order to defend himself, to cut all kinds of rope, to whittle, to hunt dinner.

When the fire was ready, I snuck out. Mom was talking on the phone inside her room. I casually walked into the living room. I took a big table lighter from the table and stuck it in my pocket. Then I went back into my room and lit the fire pile.

It didn't take the fire long to get under way. First the paper burned, then as it reached the flames it engulfed the sticks and before I knew it the fires of Hell had broken out. And smoke! My eyes stung and I was in tears. The room was full of smoke. I ran outside, coughing. Mom broke off her phone conversation and came running. The smoke was out of the bedroom door.

– What the devil have you been doing, child?

Later that day, Dad came home. I knew it was because of the fire. I knew why he had come. I had a knot in my stomach. I tried to breathe but I couldn't fill my lungs.

It's terrible being spanked. I tried to stick against the bed and hide my butt from him. But he was stronger than me. He picked me up in his hands and put me over his knees.

My tears fell freely. My heart was thrashing about like it wanted to rip itself out of my chest and escape: to climb up the bookshelves and sit there, or to run all the way, in one burst, to Aunt Salla's house.

I fought tooth and nail and cried like a condemned man:

- I'll never do it again! I'll never do it again, I'll never do it again!

X

His aggression frequently vents itself quite
directly, though when he's stuck in a hole he tends
to find it more advisable to run and hide […] He
is exceedingly simple in the way he identifies with
others' lives and experiences […] To help deal
with his anxiety and unpleasant feelings, the boy
employs denial, albeit sometimes with good reason.
Also, he tries to escape or avoid discomforting or
anxiety-inducing situations, often through a quite
mechanical restlessness in his behavior.

(National Hospital, Psychiatric Ward,
Children's Hospital Trust, 09/05/1972)

There's a bad smell in my room, a sour, burned smell. It lasts for many weeks. There is a huge burned spot on the carpet. A monument to yet another defeat for the Indians in the ruthless world of the white man.

I go out of my room. Mom is setting coffee cups and plates on the kitchen table. They are for visiting guests, clearly for people we know. Family and friends drink coffee in the kitchen. Only strangers get coffee in the living room. And only strangers get to drink coffee from the fancy cups.

- Who's coming? I ask.

- No one in particular.

She sets out cake forks for the Christmas *randalín*.

- Who's coming? I ask again.

- The girls are just coming to get made up, she replies.

It's fun to put on makeup. Mom's girlfriends, her sisters, come over to visit. And they get made-up. Mom laughs and is happy. I like seeing her happy. It happens all too rarely. Usually she's just tired. But not when she does makeup. That's always good fun.

Mom doesn't say much when she's at home with just Dad and me. Mom and Dad rarely talk, except when they argue about bridge. They play bridge on Monday evenings. When they come home, they're arguing. I hear the quarrel until I fall asleep.

- Why did you say Three No Trumps on that hand, idiot! What gave you that idea? You must trust your partner!

- That hasn't worked out in the past, though.

- And the round before that—what were you playing at?

- I had a decent hand of clubs.

- Why didn't you lead, then, with clubs?

- Oh, so you think that would have made sense?

- Yes, at least it would have worked!

The doorbell rings. I know now that you don't say "tinkles." Stebbi's mother taught me that. She often corrects me. She taught me that one "rings" a doorbell but doesn't "tinkle" it. But you can tinkle a bell that's on a table.

Gunna has arrived. She's Mom's sister. She's fat and large. She's a hoot. It's like she's a guy. She belches without putting her hand over her mouth. She farts, too, so everyone can hear; it's freaking hilarious.

- I've got awful gas!

She talks loudly and sometimes says something funny that I don't always get. I like, though, the way she says things. Sometimes she says something funny to my Dad when he's grumbling about something boring like smoking or something someone said on the radio.

- Are you still smoking, Gunna?

- Why the dickens do you care?

- Didn't you promise me you'd stop?

- I've never promised you anything.

Dad doesn't know what to say to that.

Once she looked at me and said to my mother:

- The boy's hung like a horse!

They looked at me and laughed. I didn't know what it meant, but it was still a pleasure. It meant that there was something good about me. I wasn't just a problem. Maybe I was incredibly tough. And it was fun to see everyone laughing, especially my mother.

Aunt Salla is here, too. She's also my mom's sister. She's the eldest. She's thin and has creased features. I like her best of all. She's always nice to me.

Before we moved to Fossvogur suburb, we lived on Skipholt, on the top floor. During the day, Mom would take me out into the yard and tie me to a pole with a long rope, so that I could play in the garden but wouldn't get too far away. I was little. But I worked out how to untie the rope. And I tried to run away to Aunt Salla's home. At one point, the police stopped me because I was trailing this very long rope behind me. They asked me where I lived, but I wouldn't tell them. I just wanted them to leave me alone so I could go to Salla's. However, they put me in a police car and took me down to the police station. A very nice woman there gave me donuts.

I was just settling down and preparing to spend some time there when my father came past and noticed me. He was astonished. He was at work and didn't know what I'd been up to.

– Isn't that my kid? he asked.

Things are always fun around Salla. She gives me treats. Her house smells good, and behind it there's a massive park with a playground.

She also has a large, black elephant made of stone; he's friends with Action Man. When Salla's niece comes to visit, she always gives me candy. Sometimes she gives me toys, too, even if it's not my birthday.

One time she gave me a metal plane. It was very cool. You could see the faces of the passengers through the windows. The aircraft had wind-up wheels and could drive itself along the floor. But planes don't drive. They're meant to fly. So I took it to the top of the apartment block that was being built close by. I often went there secretly. I knew it was forbidden, but I didn't care. It wasn't someone's home so I wasn't disturbing people.

I enjoyed climbing the scaffolding and throwing things off the roof. But you have to be careful when you are very high up on a roof: if you fall then you can die.

Once I did fall. But it was okay because I just hit the scaffolding below. I hurt myself, but not much. At least, I didn't die. The Lone Ranger has often fallen down and has even hurt himself badly.

I played with the airplane for a while. It was going to fly to Trondheim, Norway, where my sister Kristín lives. All the passengers were very excited and felt happy to be going abroad. They all wanted to go to Duty-Free and buy salt licorice and PK-chewing gum. Then they were going to go see the cathedral in Trondheim.

I took a running start and threw the plane high up in the air, off the roof. The passengers grinned because they were airborne.

The aircraft completed many circles in the sky before it fell to the ground.

I ran down.

It had landed in a heap. The wheels had broken off. It was a plane crash, and in all plane crashes, the planes catch fire.

I had some matches on me. I piled rubbish around the fuselage and set fire to it. The paint on the plane scorched. The merry faces of the passengers melted and turned into black blobs. No one survived.

I wish I'd had some bombs. Sometimes, after New Year's Eve fireworks, I have bombs. I stuff them into toys and light them.

It would have been fun to see the plane explode in the air and come apart.

Jón Gunnar's problems increase innumerably. He is heedless, incautious, seems never to learn anything from experience. He is isolated from his group of friends, yet always wants to be in charge and uses any means at his disposal to become their leader, even damaging their toys. He can, however, on several occasions appear quite normal if just with one child at a time, especially indoors. The boy's imagination is boundless—he's always off in some other world—though he doesn't especially suffer any distress from this. He is very careless about his things, as though nothing really matters to him. He doesn't have a lot of fear; after the parents discussed it at length between themselves, they agreed that what had affected him most in the last two years were some scenes from children's shows on TV. The parents find it very troublesome that he tends to have difficulty concentrating.

(National Hospital, Psychiatric Ward,
Children's Hospital Trust, 02/04/1972)

All the women sit in the kitchen and talk. They talk about their jobs and some friends and what's on their mind.

They tell stories about the old days. I love hearing how everything was in the old days. Back then, everyone was always drunk and lived in turf houses. Also, everyone was really poor and when they went to the movies they ate raisins instead of popcorn.

The women also know tons of stories about people who were total dumbasses as children. One woman, for example, kept peeing herself, even after she'd become a teenager. My mom looked after her and tried to break the habit by making her smell her panties whenever she peed herself. That would make her start to cry. Mom did an impression of her:

– Dob't bake me smell dem, Gútta, dob't bake me smell!

But Mom made her sniff her pissy clothes; eventually, she broke the habit, married some guy, and moved to Australia.

Another woman had a speech impediment and couldn't say *arr* or *ess* until she was an adult.

– Hi, my name is Thalla Kwithtinthdóttiw!

They're fascinating stories. The aunts talk animatedly and mimic people. And then they laugh.

Sometimes, though, they talk about serious things; they know all kinds of horror stories. Some are about people who have gotten injured and died or become cripples. And usually people are injured when they're least able to afford it, so it's an especially hard blow for everyone. People are always carefree and merry at the beginning of such stories, but their world comes crashing down in a single moment.

The moral of these stories is that, just because you think that everything is OK, and it definitely seems to be it, actually it often isn't.

You lower your voice when telling such stories.

They also know stories that make my skin squirm a bit, stories about women who have gotten pregnant and had a baby which at first seemed okay, but then they began to suspect that something wasn't right. Everyone told them that everything was fine and they were worrying unnecessarily.

– But she didn't feel right...

And in the end, I always found out that the child was blind, or handicapped, or both.

– She said: Something's wrong with the baby. No one else saw anything worth checking into. But they took it to the doctor and he looked at it and then it came out...

– It was a mango!

– Exactly. Because she was so old when she gave birth.

– But he's very nice. Always tidy and clean.

Yeah, exactly. Mangos are usually harmless.

Salla doesn't say Mong, but mango, like the fruit.

– Like when Halli and Áslaug had that boy...

– That was horrible!

– Yes, it must be awful to have such a deformed child.

– Tragic.

– It didn't have any eyes! Then again, better that than to be stillborn.

They all nod and nod.

They know so many of these stories. And they know how to tell them. I stand at a distance, drinking in each and every word. It's like the words are glue; they fix me there.

Some of the stories I've heard so many times I've got them memorized. But I still love hearing them again.

One story is about a little girl who was always biting other kids. Her mother was completely at a loss what to do, until she said to her:

– If you bite, I'll hit you in the mouth.

And the next time the girl bit someone, the mother struck her on the mouth so hard it bled.

– But she never bit anyone again after that!

By far the most serious stories are about cancer. That's very serious. Cancer is a very dangerous disease. It makes people get terribly weak and when Mom goes to visit them in the hospital then they've got skeletal faces and it's like a concentration camp.

– There was nothing left of him, just skin and bones. It was horrible to see him.

– Just like a concentration camp!

Then people die, and it's better to die than to live with cancer. It's "good to go."

I don't find the cancer stories entertaining. I hope I never get cancer.

While they share stories, they drink coffee and smoke. Mom smokes Winstons. Salla smokes Viceroys, and Gunna smokes Camels.

I like Salla's cigarettes best of all because she keeps them in a leather case. Indians keep things in leather cases.

When they talk, they also use words that no one else uses. It's womanspeak. It's like a code, like they don't want anyone else to understand what they are saying. Stebbi and I sometimes use cryptography in our tribe of Indians. We use a notebook from the Landbank. The notebook is a little book you get when you open an account, a sort of booklet with saving tips. You can write all kinds of memos in the notebook. Cryptography is very cool. Each character has a specific symbol. Jón is written like this:

My mom sometimes uses strange, made-up words. If someone is angry, then he is *foj*. When I'm sick, she says I'm *sloj*. If I'm not sick, but am coming down with something, then I'm *dommara*-like.

- Is the boy ill?
- Yes, something's laid him low.
- Is he *sloj*?
- Well, he's burning up.

If something is absolute crap, it's simply *moj*. And they know odder words, too. It's fun to listen to them talk.

- Is that a new coat?
- Yes, thanks for noticing. Isn't it *lekker*?
- Very smart.
- Gunnar got it for me from London.
- That's quite a fancy coat.
- Both for special occasions and everyday.
- Isn't it too long?
- That's the fashion!

I'm never fashionable. The clothes I wear are principally durable.

- Well, the boy's wearing fine pants.

- Yes, I got them from the megastore, Hagkaup.

- Aren't they great?

- Yes, they're very durable.

- Hagkaup has terrific stuff. And so cheap!

- He always rips the knees.

My pants are called Duffy's; they're blue jeans. Mom bought them on sale in Hagkaup. I have several pairs. I like wearing jeans. I also have corduroy pants. I'd rather wear jeans than corduroy. Indians can wear jeans if they aren't wearing Indian pants. But no Indian goes around in corduroy.

They start in on the makeup. Mom stirs black mud in a coffee cup.

First they put rollers in their hair, then styling gel. Sometimes they also paint their nails. When they do, there's a very peculiar and pungent odor.

They tilt their heads back. Mom puts cotton patches over the sisters' eyes and then black mud on their eyelashes with a cotton bud. All the while they smoke and chat. They talk more loudly when their eyes are closed, as if they think that people hear worse with closed eyes. Gunna tells the story of an irritating woman who is working with her at The Sausage Folk. Mom and Salla know the woman and also find her annoying.

- She's always being a *tizpot* about something!

- She's naturally disappointed with things.

- What is it with her?

- She's such a *pickywitch*.

- Snobbery, plain and simple, that's the way with these people.

I've been to The Sausage Folk. They make hot dogs there. I went there with my mom one time to visit Gunna and Salla. It smelled very strange and everyone was wearing white aprons, white shoes, and hats.

On the way home, I tried to give Mom the slip and go down to the beach. I was too little to go on my own. Mom noticed what I was up to and held onto the hood of my coat so I couldn't run off.

Every time before we would go into town, Mom would talk to me and tell me that I had to act calmly. Every time, I promised. But then I would forget myself. There were so many things I just had to see. Sometimes I saw weird people I wanted to go and talk to.

It was fun to go into town and run. Mom would run after me. It was like being in a chase. And it was incredibly exciting to run away and hide and make Mom look for me.

Once, I hid myself under a car. Mom was right next to me and called for me. It was incredibly exciting. She saw me, though, when the car drove off. I was so scared I started crying and my mom saw where I was lying, weeping on the road. She became very angry. She was angry because she was scared and I had nearly been seriously hurt.

She was often angry...but weren't we just playing?

She also often took me on the bus. I had to sit next to her by the window. Mom wanted me to spend more time watching what was going on outside, but I was thinking about things that were going on inside the bus. I imagined I was an Indian who was headed to prison. And when my mom wasn't looking, I'd climb over the seat and make for the back of the bus. Sometimes, I'd run off the bus when it was at a stop, somewhere out in the middle of nowhere. I'd hide myself, and wait for Mom to find me. And sometimes I was in the same place for a long, long time. Indians are good at waiting and hiding. Sometimes, though, Mom didn't come and I didn't hear her calling for me.

I'd realize I didn't know where I was, and I would get scared and start crying and call for my mom. Usually some people I didn't know would come and try to help me. Then Mom would come. She was pretty much always upset.

I wasn't allowed to talk on the bus. Not to my mother, and not to strangers. And I had to promise not to before we got on the bus.

– You'll sit still and be quiet, understand?

– Yes.

But then I just had to talk.

– Mom? What sort of house is that? Look, look, Mom, an ambulance! Perhaps Grandma is dead! Should we go and check?

Mom didn't answer; she shushed me. I'd try talking to other people. I wanted to know people's names, where they lived, what their favorite food was. Mom called it chatter.

– You shouldn't chatter at people like this.

Sometimes I'd tell people about myself, what my name is, where I live and how old I am. I'm not rude to anyone. Except to people who looked annoying or who were rude. I was sometimes rude in response.

– Do you screw a lot?

That gets people worked up. It's hilarious.

But my mom would get mad at me. I thought that was really unfair. I felt she should be mad at the people who were being rude to a little boy. Rude people shouldn't be allowed to go into town or on the bus. They should stay at home, in pajamas, until they promise to stop being rude.

The doctor said I couldn't suggest this kind of thing to Mom.

– Do you realize that it makes your mother sick and tired if you keep suddenly running away from her?

- We're just playing.

- Don't you have friends to play with?

- I'm an Indian. I'm in a tribe of Indians.

The doctor told Mom to punish me for being naughty by making me go to bed. And the next time we went to town, she reminded me about that.

- Don't run away from me and don't chatter at people you see. Promise?

- Yes.

- And you have to sit next to me on the bus and be well-behaved and calm.

- Yes.

- If you start being naughty, we'll go home and you'll go straight to bed and you won't get to watch TV.

The main challenge is that boy has been difficult
for a long time, and has been growing more and
more so, since he was about 2½ years old. He has
become vehement in all respects, unbridled in both
his delight and his misery, inconsiderate and
demanding, out of control and confused; this is
true both when he is outside his home, for example
on the bus or in a shop, and also at times when
guests come to his home. He is alienated from other
children and can be really coarse in his language.

I watch a lot of TV. I watch *Bonanza* and *The Latest*. I also watch *Our Hour*.

Dad watches the news. From time to time, he watches talk shows. I'm not allowed to bother him then. But often I have to ask him about something before I forget.

Sometimes, Dad comes home from work and starts watching the news right away. It's possible I haven't seen him for days. And perhaps I have something especially interesting that I simply must tell him. So I sneak up to him and try to whisper it. He doesn't even look at me, just stares at the news. If I speak more loudly, he raises the volume on the TV, and then I have to shout so he can hear me.

– "THE SUPREME COURT IN STUTTGART YESTERDAY SENTENCED THE TERRORISTS ANDREAS BAADER AND GUDRUN ENSSLIN FOR THEIR PURSUIT OF TERRORIST ACTIVITIES..."

– Dad!

– "THE RED BRIGADES ARE..."

– DAD!

He doesn't look at me. Sometimes I try to turn his face from the TV so it faces me. Then he gets irritated and pushes me away.

– Mom! Take the kid.

Then Mom comes to fetch me and take me away.

– You mustn't bother your dad when he's watching TV.

– But I was just telling him...

– You mustn't bother him.

– Can't I ask him just one thing?

– No.

I never really see my dad. He works so much. He leaves early in the morning and comes home late at night. Then he flops down and watches the news on TV or listens to it on the radio in the kitchen.

I'm not allowed to disturb him then. I'm not allowed to disturb him, either, when he's working on something around the home. I get in his way and he becomes exasperated.

– Don't touch that. Leave it be! It's dangerous!

– What is it?

– Leave it be.

The father is dark haired, broad-shouldered,
of medium height. He appears fairly warm, a man
of conviction; like his wife, however, he has
considerable difficulty expressing himself. He
downplays the boy's problems; what's more, he
says that he isn't as aware of them as his wife
is, and he was able to maintain that this visit
was less a concern to him than to his wife.

(National Hospital, Psychiatric Ward,
Children's Hospital Trust, 08/02/1972)

That summer, Dad goes out to the country and I'm not allowed to go with him. When he comes back he has pictures of himself and all these people I don't know. It's good weather, sunny and really nice. Everyone is always happy. Sometimes, the people in the pictures are messing around with each other and laughing, their mouths open. In some of the pictures my dad is holding some small boys. The boys are friendly towards him and call him Grandpa. Dad evidently feels very fond of these boys.

None of them have red hair.

△

I give Mom the slip in town. I run into a yard and climb far up a tree. She finds me. She tells me to come down right this minute. She can't climb. She doesn't speak loudly because there are people watching. But she is firm and she whispers as loudly as she can.

- Will you come down right now!

Suddenly I feel like I'm Tarzan. I've seen heaps of Tarzan films: *Tarzan and the Dwarves*, *Tarzan and the Lost City*. Tarzan travels by swinging between trees. He jumps between the branches or swings across by hand. He's very strong. I'm strong, too. I'm stronger than all the boys in my year. There's only one boy in the whole school who's stronger than me.

Everyone is looking at me. It's great. It's like the gathering crowd is the audience at the cinema watching a Tarzan film. I'm Tarzan. A man walks up to the tree.

- Why don't I fetch your boy down?

Mom smiles awkwardly.

- I'm at a loss what to do.

He's going to come get me. There's another tree at the same height as this tree I'm in. I climb higher. The man climbs the tree.

- Come on, kid. Enough messing around.

Without thinking about it, I jump away from my spot towards a branch. I'm Tarzan. I'm going to leap over to the other tree and swing between the branches.

But I'm not able to get a hold. The branch is soft and bends under my weight. I'm slipping. I try to grab the branch above me but I can't reach it. I grope about in the air. I hear my mother calling.

– Jón Gunnar!

I slam onto my back. It's bad. I can't breathe. I try to cry but I can't do that, either. People come running.

– Is he all right?

– I've never seen anything like it!

Mom gets me to my feet. I'm relieved to find that I'm okay. Mom thanks the man for trying to rescue me. Then she hurries me away.

– What on earth were you thinking, playing around like that?

– I don't know.

– No, you don't know. I can't think for you. I can't run everywhere right behind you. I'm exhausted.

She puts me to bed as soon as we get home. Even though it's still daytime. She puts me in my pajamas and takes away my Legos.

– Do you know why I'm doing this? she asks.

I don't know.

– Because you were naughty. I told you that if you were naughty then I would put you straight to bed.

– But I've finished being naughty.

– But because you were, you have to go to bed.

When I come back out to watch *Bonanza* she chases me back in.

– I'm not naughty.

– You were naughty, so you've got to stay inside your room!

– I've stopped that now.

– Stay in your room.

– But, Mom! *Bonanza*!

- You should have thought about that before you decided to be naughty.

Mom was very determined. I'd finished being naughty. I was really calm. I didn't understand why I couldn't watch *Bonanza*. So I snuck out. I was trying to sneak past Mom and into the TV room. She saw me and she had this really angry expression. I ran back into my room. I didn't understand why she was so pissed. I couldn't watch *Bonanza* and it wasn't fair. I opened the door and called out.

- I promise I'll behave.

Mom didn't answer. She was angry. I started to wail.

- I'll never do it again, Mom. I'll never do it again!

✕

The mother is heavy-set and lumbering; she often
sighs sadly and has difficulty explaining why she
is so tired, or in fully discussing her depressive
condition. Her skin has sallowed, especially
visible in the dark circles under her eyes. She has
a limited vocabulary, speaks in short sentences,
and often seems like she doesn't know how to match
words and things, which made it especially tricky
to get the story of their daily lives or indeed to
get her to list specific aspects or symptoms of the
boy's behavior. She asked in each interview about
the outcome of the study, and then seemed wholly
concerned about her own anxiety and impatience.

(National Hospital, Psychiatric Ward,
Children's Hospital Trust, 08/02/1972)

✕

Mom gives the women beer in brown bottles. She makes it herself. It has a very strange smell to it, sweet and bitter at the same time. They smoke.

- Have Olla and Stebbi moved? asks Mom.

- Yes, they moved over the weekend, answers Salla.

- It's a really great apartment, says Mom. I hope it goes well for them, she adds.

- He's a very hard-working man, says Salla.

- Shame about her, adds Gunna.

- She's not a bad person, says Mom.

Gunna shakes her head, and takes a big drag of her cigarette.

- I don't give a toss whether she's good or bad; she's a drunkard!

- She's always been delicate, Salla says.

- An emotional person, adds Mom.

- I think she's just a waste of space, Gunna declares.

- Don't say that, Gunna, says Salla.

- I'll say it if I want to! She's a drunken wretch.

- That's true, Mom says. She does drink a lot, often. But she's never been addicted to pills.

Salla agrees, wholeheartedly. Gunna tuts, and moves the conversation on Mom closes the curtain over the kitchen window. The sisters head over to the oven; they're only wearing their bras. They wash their hair in the kitchen sink. Then they sit back down at the kitchen table, comb each other's hair and put rollers in.

After that, they move to the living room to dry their hair. They sit next to one another on the couch, each with their own hairdryer. The hairdryers are white and called Rowenta. Coming out of each hairdryer is a little pipe with a colorful plastic cap they put over their hair. When they turn on the hairdryer, hot air flows through the pipe and into the plastic cap, which expands. The caps have small holes so they don't explode. Mom has a yellow cap with flowers on it. Gunna has a monochrome brown cap, and Salla's is pink, decorated with pink flowers. The sound of the hair dryers is like the sound of the vacuum cleaner.

I watch them with affection and respect. These women are the most perfect and intriguing people I know. They know everything, and have all the answers.

I go back to my room. I feel good. It's nice to see my mom so happy.

Inside the living room, the sisters are sitting side by side on the couch with their colorful air-helmets on their heads, smoking and drinking coffee, yelling to each other so they're not drowned out by the noisy roar.

My school is called Foxvox School. I don't really enjoy school and I find it hard to sit still. I can sit for a while but then I have to move or change position. I also find it difficult when I can't talk the way I want to.

But I like homeroom. Each class goes to their own room. We sit on a soft rug while the teacher talks to us and asks us questions. I get to talk a lot. I like talking and telling funny stories. Sometimes I can't control myself and simply have to talk. Those times, I interrupt. I also like to repeat words someone else has said. But I'll say them a bit different. I think it's fun to rhyme words, too. If someone says a strange word then I'll rhyme it with another word. For example, if someone says "stapler," I'll say "mapler."

Most rhyming words are nonsense, but not all. If someone says "tree" then perhaps I'll say "knee."

Some words I also just like saying over and over again and hearing how they sound. I like "toddler," for example, a really good word. I never tire of saying it. "Toddler."

My teacher calls this chat. She doesn't like it when I rhyme or repeat words. She doesn't think it's fun and she thinks I'm teasing people. But I'm not. I don't know why I do it. The words repeat over and over inside my head; I get them in my brain and cannot get them out except by saying them out loud. But it's stupid and that's why I make like I'm kidding intentionally.

I also love words that don't exist and don't mean anything. "Jarrydust" is one of these words. "Splunderer" is another. I say them sometimes when I don't know what to say. I love to say these words. They're funny words.

– Jón, what's a subjunctive?

– Err, a splunderer?

– Stop being silly.

– Jarrydust?

– Jón, who wrote the story of *The Ugly Duckling*?

– Donald Duck?

Everyone laughs. It's better to be a comic than a moron.

Sometimes the teacher asks the class questions nobody knows the answer to but me. I like that a lot.

– Children, do you know what the offspring of bears are called?

A few put their hands up. Me too.

– Puppies?

The teacher shakes her head.

– Little bears?

– No.

Finally I'm the only one left. The teacher looks at me and nods.

– Cubbyholes!

Everyone laughs. That was funny. But it's also true. They're called cubs. I like to mix words together to create nonsense.

The teacher smiles and nods. She's called Svandís and is very strict. Sometimes she pinches my neck with her nails when I'm naughty. I try to be careful about needling her.

Some teachers are fun to tease. I enjoy messing with them. But some teachers are annoying.

One time, I was telling a story about a little kid who peed before he reached the bathroom.

– Did he pee over himself? asked the teacher.

I told her that it's wrong to say that someone has peed *over* themselves. It's not possible to pee *over* yourself. You should just say that someone peed themselves. She got very annoyed and said I was being impertinent. But I wasn't. I know that one shouldn't bullshit adults.

When I was a kid I would sometimes hide from teachers. I liked doing that a lot but I've grown out of it now. I'm not as naughty as I used to be. I also don't feel as bad as I felt then. Back then, I had no friends and I was afraid of the other kids.

When I first started school, I thought I was going to die. Mom had to go with me every morning because I didn't want to go. I was terrified. Gradually, however, I began to feel better. I got to know the kids and discovered that most of them are okay. Though there are some older kids who are annoying and who pick on me during recess. They follow me home and also sometimes call me Coppertop Brennivínsson.

When I know they're planning to follow me home, I prepare. Sometimes I put big stones in my pockets. When they arrive and begin to tease me, I try to throw stones at their heads. Then they get frightened and run away, yelling:

– He's crazy, he's a lunatic!

I've still never hit anyone. I just want to scare them.

Sometimes I do have to fight. But I've not hit any one, not properly. They're just scuffles. I don't want to hurt anyone, except when I am very angry.

I've only once beaten up a kid at school on purpose. There was a kid who was always teasing me, jostling me and tripping me and calling me Coppertop Brennivínsson. He would get at me during recess and sometimes follow me home and try to trip me up if we ran into each other in the school corridor. He's two years older than me. Everyone thinks he's a jerk.

Shortly before it happened, I'd broken my arm on my bike. I had just gotten a speedometer and I was trying to set a speed record; I rode so fast down a steep hill that I lost control of the bike and hit a pole.

I had to go to the emergency room and get a plaster cast.

The boy came over to me during recess and wanted to see the cast. When he was standing right beside me I hit him really hard in the head with the cast.

He began to scream. It suited him. I liked seeing him screaming. He had annoyed me so many times. And when he was starting to attack me, a teacher came and took him by the scruff of the neck, and marched him to the principal.

A little bit later, the teacher came back and got me and took me to the principal. The principal had me apologize to the boy for having smacked him and then he apologized to me for having teased me and promised never to do that again. He kept his promise. I was really happy to see him cry. You can't tease someone who has seen you cry.

I often go to the principal. Teachers take me there when they've had enough of me and are ready to give up. Sometimes, I have to go to him even though I haven't done anything bad. But that's okay because the principal is a good guy. He never scolds me. He talks to me gently. Sometimes he gives me chocolate milk and even a Prince Polo candy bar.

Once, I beat up a teacher. It wasn't something I planned. It was when I was littler. I was hiding so I climbed up on the big shelf above the classroom door. I imagined that I was an Indian lying in wait, and the teacher was a cowboy who would kill me if she found me.

The teacher walked around the school from end to end, searching for me and calling me. She had long, raven-black hair, which reached all the way down to her butt.

I was teasing her by sometimes answering her.

– I'm here, inside the homeroom!

Then I'd stifle my giggles when she came in. I could see her but she couldn't see me. She never looked up. One of the times she walked through the door I jumped down towards her.

I don't know what happened. I did it without thinking. I was just planning to shock her. But she was much more irate than I reckoned. As I fell, I groped the air and grabbed hold of her hair. We both fell to the floor.

I hurt her. She had to have a collar around her neck. That time, the principal got angry with me. He said she had been lucky not to have broken her neck. I realized this with hindsight and so I began to cry. I begged for her forgiveness. I didn't mean to hurt her.

I often do things I only understand in hindsight. At the time, I don't know why I do them. One moment, I'm thinking something and then it's like I'm not thinking anything and all of a sudden I have to do something. Some of those times, someone gets angry with me, and I cry because I realize.

◉

The study has revealed that the boy is very
intelligent indeed, more than capable, with a
highly developed sense of his own independence—
nevertheless, he also seeks, like an infant, to
have his needs for food and warmth met. His need
for a safe and warm refuge or hiding place conflicts with his desire to go on adventures and to
be self-sufficient. Along with a need for intimate
and tactile relationships can be seen both fear
and resentment towards adult figures, and rebellion
against their rule. Jón Gunnar experiences himself as imperfect and even castrated. Often, he has
doubts about his abilities, which may manifest as
oppositional behavior, because it is better not to
want than not to get. His emotional adaptability is
poorly developed. He has difficulty controlling his
emotions: his need for power and for gratification
cannot be deferred. He is aware of the needs his
surroundings bring out in him, and when those needs
clash with his internal desires, it causes conflict
and turmoil.

(National Hospital, Psychiatric Ward,
Children's Hospital Trust, 09/05/1972)

JÓN GNARR

I don't have any enemies at school because I don't get into fights. However, there's usually a lot of fighting at recess and some kids are always being picked on. There are kids who are strange, behave weird, or dress in silly ways.

One girl, who is called Mental Gunna, always starts crying when she's teased. She is often all alone, talking to herself. She really is mental. Sometimes lots of kids club around her and tease her until she starts crying. I think it's sick. I'd never do that.

They're all always teasing this boy in the class they call Rubber Tarzan, like the character in the book by Ole Lund Kirkegaard. Sometimes someone spits in their palm, and tells him to eat the spittle. And he does. Then they all start laughing, and he does, too. It's like he hasn't figured out they're making fun of him.

My friends at school aren't necessarily my friends at home. I play with most of the kids in my street. My best friend is Kristján Þór. He's also my cousin. He doesn't have any friends but me. We're always together. We play Legos and Action Man. Kristján Þór is in my class, too. I mostly stopped playing with Stebbi when I started hanging out with Kristján Þór. Other classmates are more like acquaintances, with whom I only play occasionally. Most of them are always practicing soccer. I don't enjoy soccer except in small doses. I'd never go to soccer practice. I don't get it, and can't ever score. Soccer is a difficult and complicated game: I never know what to do until long after I'm supposed to do it. And so no one wants to be on my team.

I'd rather have a snowball fight or play chase during recess than soccer. I do have a Liverpool FC bag and support Liverpool but that's more to side with others.

I find it annoying being at school when the weather's good. Those days, I'd rather be outside playing. I think it is unfair to have school during good weather or excellent amounts of snow.

I'm no good at learning. The teacher is always telling me to quit making noise.

– Less chit-chat, Jón!

I think chit-chat is a funny word. I make a lot of chit-chat. I like to rhyme it.

– Kit chit-chats with Nat, Nat chit-chats with Kit, Kit and Nat chit-chat...

– Shush!

Sometimes the teacher sits me away from the other kids, so I'm not bothering them; she sits with me and makes me study. I don't learn much, even then. Everything is too hard.

My school is an open school. There are no classrooms; instead, everyone learns together in an open space or goes to their home-room. You don't get grades like in other schools but instead you're given comments. You can get Good, Decent, or Fair. Good is best. Yet it really means the same thing as Decent. But in the old days it was different: Good meant best of all. I don't ever get G in any of my comments. I'm typically given D. Then usually an explanation: Slow progress. Often makes a racket. Disturbs other children.

I find schoolbooks the worst books in the world. They're difficult. It is like they're made to be annoying. I get a pain in my forehead from looking at them. Even the pictures in them are annoying. I don't follow them and I don't want to learn about them. I only ever enjoy them if there are stories.

I get a sense of suffocation from learning. I get the same feeling when I'm forced to learn as I do when I'm forced to eat food I find disgusting.

I try to avoid learning at home. I always tell my mom that I learned everything I need to learn at school. Sometimes she believes me or doesn't feel like chasing me but sometimes she makes me study in my room and sits over me and I don't get to go until I'm done with the things I've got to do.

I have to practice handwriting. It sucks. I have to write the same letter over and over again. I can't write the letters so that they fit in the lines. They're usually either too small or too large, or too fat or even too skinny. They're nothing like letters.

I write ugly. I don't enjoy what I'm writing because it's so ugly and stupid. I can't write in a straight line so what I write always slopes down and even goes onto the line below.

No one in my class writes as badly as I do.

△

Jón Gunnar is a 5-year old boy whose parents came to the ward because of his behavioral problems. They say he displays violence, is compulsive, has an obscene vocabulary, doesn't take care of his toys, has no sense of time and space and has difficulty concentrating. Furthermore, he finds it impossible to write the letter J correctly.

(National Hospital, Psychiatric Ward,
Children's Hospital Trust, 09/05/1972)

He is very cocksure of himself, quickly deciding
he wants to draw for me, but not doing so very
successfully; he doesn't seem fully in control
of his imagination. Next he draws all the letters
in the alphabet that are important, and that is I,
an inverted J, and A. His parents emphasize that
it is impossible to teach him to write J correctly.

(National Hospital, Psychiatric Ward,
Children's Hospital Trust, 02/04/1972)

Grammar is also incredibly difficult and frustrating. You have to decline words and know what sort of words they are. Some are nouns and some are adjectives. And then there are particles and adverbs. I can't remember the difference between them and always muddle them together. I also don't care. I don't want to learn about this. I don't think I need it.

In my school, there are no exams. Instead, we have quizzes. When there is a grammar quiz, I try to do as well as I can. But I still make lots of errors, especially with adverbs and particles, but also with the other things. I mainly guess. Most of what I get right is not because I know the rules but because I remember how the word looks or else I just guess right.

JÓN GNARR

Spelling is more difficult. You have to learn the rules of how words are written. I find all the rules annoying, especially the y/ý-rule. If it was up to me, then I wouldn't have an ypsilon. You can't hear the difference when people are talking.

When I read, I look carefully at the words and try to remember their shapes. That's the best way I can remember how they're written, since I don't know the rules. I've no idea, for example, why a person writes Christ and not Cryst, the way you say it, or wonder instead of wander. But I remember, so it doesn't matter.

Math is the most difficult of all. If there is one thing I wouldn't have to learn, that's it. I'm so far behind in it. Other kids are beginning to learn division but I'm still in subtraction. I only know the easiest things. I don't know how to carry over. I can't ever remember how it's done.

Most people know all the times tables. I only know one times and two times and ten times tables. When I'm studying math, it's like the numbers are made of little parts that run about in all directions as soon as I look at them.

I find nothing in the world as frustrating as math. I find it more frustrating than sitting on a hard bench at a funeral, in too-tight shoes and my best clothes, which scratch and itch all over. When I study math, I feel like I'm choking, like it's drowning my soul.

I can't learn examples. Mom sometimes sits with me and explains the rules. I don't understand them. I don't want to understand them. I don't hear what she says. I just nod my head and pretend to listen and look where she tells me to look. Then when I do it myself, I try to work out from her reactions what's right.

– And what's the answer, then?

I focus on the example like I understand it a hundred percent.

- Ehhh...seven?

- No.

- Five?

- No, you borrowed.

I make a sound like I'm finally realizing it.

- Yes! Ehhh...nine ?

I often guess nine because it is the hardest number, nine or seven. My favorite number is eight. That's because it's made of two rings, and its fun to write. I also like to write five. I see numbers like dots on a dice and think about them that way. That's why seven and nine are so difficult, perhaps: I don't ever see them.

- Jón!

- Yes!

I act like it's totally unnecessary to get all worked up: I understand it all completely. But in reality I'm lost. It's like I've fallen asleep inside even though I'm awake. It often happens when I get bored or frustrated, but also when I'm trying to think about something interesting. The teacher calls that daydreaming. But it isn't always daydreaming. I know what dreaming daydreams is like; I do it all the time. But sometimes it's different. Those times, I'm not thinking anything or dreaming. I try to think but I can't. It's like the thoughts are suddenly stuck and won't come, like they're all locked inside one room. Maybe I'm just a moron.

They think I don't want to understand. I've been trying but I can't get it. It's no fun not knowing how to write or add up. It's no fun always being a total moron. It's not because I'm lazy. It's no fun to sit alone out in the corner learning subtraction for months on end or to sit with mom in my room staring at books. It would be easier to learn it and then go back outside to play. I don't want to do this, any more than I want to drink others' pee or eat lumpfish. My teacher wouldn't want to work in a workshop and always be drilling things by hand. Dad wouldn't want to stay at home knitting or putting on makeup. Why do I have to do what I don't want to, what I'm not good at? I don't understand. Everyone just says that I have to learn.

–You'll need this when you grow up.

I really doubt it. I can tell I'll never need multiplication tables. I feel it's about as important as knowing how many hairs different types of dog have or what materials my clothes are made from. It's like having to memorize a bunch of telephone numbers in case you need to call someone. If I really need to know something, I can just ask someone. Why aren't there schools for kids where there's no math and no annoying rules and just all play and telling stories? If I find I don't like the rules when I'm grown up, will I have to stick with them? I'm simply myself. Is there a place for me? I know some of the rules, even if I don't know everything. I know how to talk better than everyone else. I know plenty. I'm funny. I know how to say entertaining things. Maybe I can tell stories when I grow up. I can tell people stories and take part that way.

I'd like to be a part of things. It's just that I'm a bit weird. I'm not like the others. I'm not good at anything that's of any value.

I feel bad about myself. I don't feel good inside. I feel so bad that I get tears in my eyes when I think about it. So I don't think about it.

Everyone gets tired of me sooner or later. I can tell by the way they look at me; I see the weariness in their eyes. Mom is tired of me, the teachers are tired of me, and my friends are sometimes tired of me, too.

I'm the most tired of all. I don't like being this way. I'm somehow all crumpled inside and I can't handle it. I don't know what to do. I've gotten lost deep inside and I can't find a way out.

That's me. I'm not pretending. I'm not trying to be annoying. Why would anyone believe me? If I wasn't funny, I'd just be stupid, and no one would want to be with me. I'd be like Rubber Tarzan. I want people to like me. I want everything to be okay.

Once a week we have Materials. We go to the big workshop full of all kinds of machinery and tools.

I want to learn about all these machines. I enjoy making things. I really like the smell of trees. They have a good smell when you saw them.

Each summer I go to a construction camp where I build myself a hut. I want to learn that more and better. I want to learn to make a two-story cabin with a door that can be locked. I also want to know how to build things for my miniatures, or a house for Action Man. It'd also be good to be able to build a dovecote with nets. I'd like to keep doves. But I don't know how to build it and there's no one to help me. I've tried it but it doesn't stay up. There's so much I can't do. Hinges. And how do you hammer nails into thin sticks without splitting them? How do you stop things leaking? What sort of nails are you meant to use when? There's so much I want to learn when it comes to carpentry. If I could choose, I'd like to make a flashy sword and shield or an Indian tent. But we can't choose what we build. We don't learn anything about the machines or how to make stuff. In fact, we don't make anything. The only thing we do is to saw animals out of plywood. And we only get to choose whether we want to make a horse or cow. It's still fun, for a little while, because we get to use a band saw. But it's only fun for a short while. Most of our time is spent polishing the animal with sandpaper. That's difficult and annoying work. You have to sand the edges well, first with coarse paper and then with fine paper. The teacher is never satisfied.

- No, you have to sand it a little more.

- It's done!

- Hmm, you do need to sand it more with some fine sandpaper.

When we're finished sanding, we put some brown stain on the animal and a plate under so it can stand up.

Finally, you burn your name under the base with a special tool. That's exciting, partly because it's fun to use the tool, but also because it's a relief not to have to sand any more.

I don't know what we're allowed to do. That's so annoying. I don't learn anything but sanding plywood. You can't tell me that's something I'll need to know when I'm all grown up. A stained plywood cow is not something anyone cares about. It won't be a gift, let alone a lovely ornament. Mom would never put something like this up in her living room. I don't want this thing in my room. And there's no one I could give it to. I don't even feel like it's worth burning. It's just pointless.

The only thing that is reliably fun at school is gym. That's when we get to play games and do all kinds of exercises: climbing rope and jumping over a horse. It's really fun to play Tarzan. That's the one where you're chased but you can't touch the floor.

The sports teacher is a professional volleyball player. He does everything he can to introduce us to the world of volleyball. We often have volleyball competitions. But volleyball is a girly sport. You can't punch or hit anything but the ball. I think it sucks and I think most boys feel the same way.

It's sometimes fun in the changing room and shower after gym. First the boys get to shower, then the girls. We whip each other with towels and muck about. We take hold of our pricks, pull them back behind our balls, clamp our thighs together, and then it's like we've got pussies.

There's much teasing after gym class. It's tough for the fat kids. Fat Dóri gets a bad ride. Everyone is always making fun of him and trying to pinch him.

- Lemme pinch your rolls, Dóri.
- Leave me alone!
- Ohhh, you're so soft.
- Shut up!

Dóri has recently moved to the Fossvogur suburb. He's considered weird and therefore automatically my friend. He's also sometimes called Little Blue because there's a British cartoon on TV about an elephant whose name is Little Blue.

Dóri is a blast. His mom and dad are divorced and he's usually always alone at home, just like me. We hang out at his home a lot and make prank calls.

Some boys are shy about getting naked. They're teased a lot, too. They keep their dicks hidden and rush in and out of the shower. Sometimes, someone grabs their underwear and throws it in the shower or hides their towel.

If a person is a really big dork, he's in danger of seeing his underwear in the toilet or else someone takes it and throws it into the girls' changing room. That's the most humiliating, especially if the underwear is embarrassing, like if it has childish pictures on it. Rubber Tarzan has this happen to him all the time. He's really the only one everyone picks on. I don't think he enjoys gym.

If we're taking too long to get dressed then the shower attendant, a woman, comes to tell us off and hurry us up. She also comes in to make sure that we aren't trying to spy on the girls in the shower.

I never torment anyone. On the other hand, I don't try to intervene when others are being tormented. If I start interfering, I'll just get teased, too. Everyone gets teased at some point. All you have to do is wear stupid clothes or simply have a silly towel.

On Fridays we go to Assembly. We all sit on the floor and the principal has us sing. We sing "Bless You, the Spring is Calling You" and "By the River Öxará" and songs like that. I enjoy it. I make up nonsense words. I forget about the lyrics and try to sing the tune wrong:

> The river's got axles, tycoons eating rice,
> An erect sunshade, shit in the fields!
> Shit on the flag, poop in the Light,
> Sperm at Þingvellir and shit in the fields.
> Onward, onward, never to shit.
> Onward, onward, men and cows alike.
> Join your chewing gum bands,
> Clasp your mucky hands,
> Fight friends, defend our land!

If it sounds like I'm messing about the teacher comes running over and pinches me and takes me away. It's best if the distortion is close to the original. If so, no one can hear but those sitting near me. They all laugh, and I'm funny and entertaining.

Everything in school is a lot of fun, except for the learning.

I'd gone to the Co-op. You can get anything under the sun there. I'd gotten a little money and I wanted to buy Mom something. But all I could afford was some thread on a piece of cardboard. Still, I think my mom will be happy with it. She has a box full of all sorts of thread. All on spools. She doesn't have any thread like this. It's in a white paper bag. I want to cheer Mom up because she is always so tired.

I'm coming back from the countryside, where I've been all summer. Perhaps she's tired because I can't stay in the country any longer.

I think I've been sent home. I'm still not sure. But I sense it. After what I did.

The farm stands in a high valley, up on a hill. A river flows through the valley. Right opposite the farm is another farm; it's deserted. Behind it is a big black mountain. Directly in front of the farm there's an old dam in the river. Below the farm is another farm; a different family lives there. All around are steep slopes and high mountains.

This is "out west:" right by Bjarkalundur and Reykhólar. I've been there, too. They process the algae. They have large machines that are like tractors; they drive out to sea and pull up seaweed. Bjarkalundur is a hotel. Dad goes there in summer. I've never been.

The farmer's wife is my aunt. She's very strict.

When I first came to the farm, she was always asking me if I was mean to my grandmother and whether I didn't think it was bad to be mean to my grandmother. I know that. But I'm not mean. Grandma and I are friends. We're only playing. She enjoys it when I play around with her.

The farmer and his wife have two sons. Their names are Ingvi and Njörður.

Ingvi is the same age as me but Njörður is a teenager. He's in the Youth Club and is very good at sports. He can jump as high as he is tall, without needing a run-up. There are also several other kids out there in the country, just like me. The farm is an ordinary house. Yet there's a very weird smell there, the smell of animals.

Outside the house is a beautiful garden where the farmer's wife grows flowers. Directly opposite the house, spread throughout the farmyard, are outbuildings: a cowshed, a sheep barn, another barn.

On the farm there's a girl called Helga. Helga is the same age as me. She's lots of fun. She's not really a girl. Girls are so often prudes. But not Helga. She's exactly like a boy. It's fun to play with her.

We mostly play on the slope between the two farms. There's a little house and some fences.

The kids in the country play differently than other kids. They don't have Action Man. Instead, they play with ram's horns and bones. The horns represent sheep. If you find an unmarked horn, you get to own it by marking it with a cut, the way it's done with lambs in real life: when a lamb is born, a piece is cut from its ear and a special label is put on it. That's how the farmer knows his sheep. It's called a sheep-mark. The kids score their horns with their own unique sheep-mark. Some cut one piece, some more pieces than others can. The mark can also be a hole or a groove.

The kids keep their horns inside their homes during winter. In spring, they put all the horns together and throw them down a hill so that they scatter across a large meadow. Later in the summer, they act like shepherds. They walk across the field, looking in the tall grass and picking up their horns.

The bones are also animals. Cheekbones are cows. Sheep bones are horses. You put a yarn bundle around the bones and drag it behind you, between your feet. Small bones are dogs and cats.

I like playing these games. I don't think they're stupid. I could spend all day rooting around with farm toys, making roads, fixing the fence. Fences are made from poles and wires. There's a skill to making a beautiful fence.

There's a simple economic system on the slope. Business is conducted primarily through barter. Some things are more valuable than others and their value depends on supply and demand. What is rare is expensive and exciting. What there's plenty of is worthless.

The formal currency on the slopes is the seed of Yellow Rattle, also called moneyflower. But since everyone has so many seeds, they're actually worthless. They grow wild in the gravel through the valley.

I share the farm with Helga. We're a farm couple. The boys tease me and call us sweethearts, though we aren't. One boy tormented me by saying I'd kissed Helga. But it wasn't true. I wouldn't ever kiss her. I would rather drink a glass full of warm cow's piss than kiss a girl. We're just a farming couple who are trying to make our farm cool.

But we also play all sorts of other games. We play chase and hide-and-seek and make cars out of big cogs we mount on the end of a stick with a nail through the middle. Then we push the cogwheels in front of us, using the stick so they spin. We drive over obstacles and compete to make it to the cowshed, seeing how far we can go without getting stuck.

I don't have to work much in the countryside. But I need to lend a hand. We're made to help in the house on the farm. The vacuum cleaner frustrates me. I'm always told off for vacuuming badly. I try to do it as well as I can. When I'm done, the farmer's wife comes over and points at the floor.

- It's everywhere. This isn't a job well done.

- But I vacuumed it all.

- Are you that lazy that you don't try?

- No.

- Then you're just bat-blind, boy. The floor is covered in crumbs and fluff.

She points all around. I have to bend right down to see the crumbs.

We also have to take care of the cows. They go out to a field after the morning milking. Then you need to fetch them back again at night. We take turns doing it. When you drive a cow, you use a lash. That's a stick with a tie on it, like a whip. You never need to hit the cows because they walk of their own accord. But it's fun to do the driving. You're entrusted with a real status when you do this. It's much better than shoveling shit.

The cows are great. They're always quiet and look like they're thinking very, very, very hard. I don't reckon they think about anything other than grass. The cows are the only animals we need to care for.

In summer, the sheep are on the mountain. You don't see much of them except when they sneak into the meadow. When that happens, we need to drive them back up the mountain.

Sheep are stinking creatures. They're grumpy and run fast. They remind me of shy cats, which run away when they see someone, as if the person is going to hurt them.

There're loads of dogs on the farm. The farmer breeds dogs and sells them. He is very strict with the dogs and trains them to become good sheepdogs. His dogs are highly sought after. His best dog is called Spot. He's so good that he understands everything that's said to him. If the sheep get into the farm, the farmer tells him what to do. He listens patiently and then runs off. He does everything right.

The couple on the farm are very religious. They believe in Jesus. I don't believe in him. They're always praying.

Everyone has to pray together in the morning and say the Lord's Prayer in the evening. And you have to say grace before you can start eating. You must close your eyes and bow your head while praying.

We're not allowed to swear in the country. If we do, we have to brush our teeth with soap. I swore a few times when I first arrived but I quickly stopped. It's strange brushing your teeth with soap. The taste is disgusting. When I get home, I'm going to make Aunt Gunna brush her teeth with soap. She swears a lot. When she farts, she says:

– Bloody hell, this damn gas!

The farming couple believe in God a lot. I don't know anything about God except what Grandma has told me about him. She says he is very good and if you believe in him and are a good person you'll go to heaven when you die.

Anton says there's no life after death, that you just rot in a grave and become food for worms. I don't know what's true. I wonder why, if God exists, he never shows up. Is he hiding? What is he afraid of?

But I've never known so much praying. Once, we all had to kneel in front of a picture of Jesus that was hanging above the double bed. Then the farmer began to pray, asking God to stop the constant rain so they could sow seed. He spoke strangely, using words I'd never heard before. He spoke to God like he was his friend.

– We gather before you today, my Lord, for we are helpless in the face of the weather. You know the script of our hearts, O Lord, and our lives, and know how important it is for us to make hay. Therefore we ask you, dear Lord...

I started laughing. I tried to hold it in but I couldn't. I thought it was so silly. They were upset and made me stay all alone inside my room for ages and I wasn't allowed at tea.

The food in the country is generally nice. In the morning we get bread and porridge. It's different eating in the country than I am used to at home. Like stirring. That's thick yogurt—*skyr*—mixed with porridge. It doesn't taste bad. At teatime, we often get *klattar*; they're like pancakes, but they're made from leftover porridge. They're tasty. Sometimes, though, there are things I can't eat. I don't eat lumpfish or soured lamb. I think moss-milk is disgusting. I'd rather not eat colostrum pudding. But I have to eat it if that's what's for dinner. I'm not allowed to get up from the table until I'm finished. It's a good job there aren't ever cucumbers.

Once when it was lumpfish for dinner, I pretended to be ill. I had to drink warm sugar water. That's the most disgusting drink I've ever tasted, sick-making and too sweet.

I once had to eat soured lamb sausage, which is the most disgusting food I've ever set eyes on. It's basically fat. I cut it into small pieces to put in my mouth and swallow without chewing or tasting them at all. When I was almost done, I threw it all up again.

We sometimes get sweets sent from home. But they're taken from us and kept inside the pantry. The farmer's wife puts tiny pieces in a tub and we can have a single piece at night if we finish dinner. At the weekend, we get chewing gum, but never at any other time. I ask Ingvi what happens to the treats when we children go back home.

- I eat them at Christmas, he said.

Once a week, we take a bath. There's no hot water on the farm. When we have a bath, the water is heated in a pan and poured into the bathtub.

We bathe two by two, foot to foot. The water is so shallow that it does not reach your thighs. The first time I got a bath, I was in with Ingvi. I turned my back to him, pulled apart my butt cheeks and stuck my asshole in his face.

– Want a chocolate?

I was immediately taken out of the bath and made to stay in my room.

– I was just kidding!

– Rudeness is never a joke. You can sit here and think about it. Ask God to forgive you and teach you not to be naughty.

I don't ask God for anything. I have repeatedly asked him to change my hair, to stop me being a redhead, or at least make my hair a bit lighter. He never does anything about it. He doesn't listen to me. I think God is being very nice to everyone else instead of me. I think he never listens to me at all. And I think he also doesn't give a fuck whether it's raining in the country or not.

When the farmer's wife closes the door I swear under my breath, so she can't hear.

– Shit, crap, fuck.

I'm always getting shut in the knitting room. The only thing in there is a big knitting machine, some bobbins with yarn on them, and all kinds of different weights.

Once, we all had to go with them to their church for some ceremony or other. The farmer's wife dressed us all in half-sleeves and collars. When we got into our jackets, it felt like we were all wearing new sweaters.

The ceremony was colossally boring. We had to sit absolutely still. I'd been to church before, for funerals. They're boring. This was different, though. Some guy spoke loudly. He used strange words.

People joined in and called out in response, even stood up and groped their hands in the air.

- Hallelujah!

- Glory to the Lord!

- Blessed be His holy name!

One woman who was sitting right beside us started weeping. I've never seen a grown woman weeping, except Grandma Anna, but she was senile and confused.

I thought it was really stupid. The farmer's wife sat next to me and watched me carefully. She's like my teacher Svandís. I wanted to say something witty or call out something but I didn't dare.

Finally Ingvi went up to the guy and he submerged him in a pool. It was a little strange. After, there was a party and then we went home.

I asked Ingvi about the dunking. He told me that the guy had submerged him in the water, down in the pool, and told him to come up from the water when he saw white doves.

- Did you see any? I asked.

- No, but I said I had, or I would have drowned.

Right by the farm is a ravine. All the trash is thrown in there and burned. That's also where all the old stuff is thrown away. We can't go down there. It is highly forbidden. I still sneak off there when no one can see. The trash dump is a temptation I can't resist. I enjoy rooting around in the stuff and examining it. There are nonstop flames from a fire in a large iron barrel. I made myself a little fort and a house out of glass stuff on the far side of the ravine. Then I went to the other side and did an air raid with stones and dry clods of earth that burst when they explode. Sometimes, I make fires.

Among the stuff there's a dead ewe. There is a hole in her stomach and she's full of bustling worms. I shovel the worms into cans and put them on the fire. Then they bubble and boil in the can; the worms all split and burst.

Perhaps I'd gotten annoying. Maybe everyone else was tired of me. I don't know. I never realize it until others have gotten angry. Then I know I've probably done something. If someone is annoyed or angry then I get a heavy heart because I am afraid it's my fault.

In the rubbish dump was a large pile of tires. They were tires from cars and tractors.

I was just playing. I took the tires and made them roll down the slope into the lagoon below.

First I took a little tire and then a big one.

It was incredibly exciting to see them roll. The slope was long and steep and the tires zinged forward with great speed and jumped and skipped. They rolled a long way out on the reservoir so that water gushed in all directions.

Then I took the big tractor tires. They were the hardest. But it was also the most fun to see them roll.

The farmer got so angry that I thought he would hit me. I was so scared I started crying in front of everyone.

I wasn't trying to ruin anything. I was just playing. I had always planned to help him get his tires back. If I had really wanted to damage them, I would have burned them before I rolled them.

A few days later, they told me I had to go home. That really sucked.

◼

Finally, we reach Reykjavík.

I find Reykjavík has changed a lot since I left. It's a different color. The smell is new, strange, mysterious. There're houses I've never noticed before. I think I've been gone a long time, for many years.

Dad picks me up at the bus station. He has a new car. Dad has just bought a Mazda.

– Welcome, he says, dryly.

– Hi.

I'm shy around him. I feel like I won't be ready to meet him for many years yet. Also, he is really angry.

– Speak in Icelandic. Don't say "hi," he says.

I sit down. The car has a new smell. The plastic is still on the seats. My dad never takes it off, just lets it come off little by little.

The windows in the back are round.

We're silent. I fiddle the plastic with my finger and look out the window. When my neighborhood appears, everything still feels strange. It's like I've never been here before and have only seen pictures of this house. It's like I've gone abroad. Everything is new. When I left, it was spring. Now it's fall. The trees have grown many feet and you can't see for leaves. A new field has sprouted. The previously frozen soil has given way to thriving flowerbeds. There are new poles and traffic signs.

Time passes here without me. It's odd.

At home, I feel like I'm an unfamiliar visitor. I feel like I have to sit in the living room. I feel like I have to ask for permission to get something from the fridge or go to the bathroom. I don't belong here.

Mom's not mad at me, but she's also not all that happy. She smiles weakly and kisses me.

– Welcome home, son.

I give my mom the package. She thanks me. But it doesn't make her as happy as I had expected. Maybe I should have bought a different kind of twine, some other color.

My room is different. It's been cleaned and tidied up.

I sit on my bed.

I find it hard to breathe.

Runa is seething. She has a shoebox in her hand.

– What did you do to my dolls?

– Nothing, I mumble.

– Fuck, you're unbearable!

– What?

I know what she's talking about. Her dolls have vanished.

– What's going on? asks Mom.

– He's been snooping in my stuff. He's taken my dolls. I came by to get them.

Mom has a weary expression on her face. She wears that expression when she is completely sick and tired of my doings.

– You just have to keep an eye on your stuff. He roots through everything.

Runa turns back to me.

– Can't you just leave my stuff alone?

– Yes, sure, I say.

– Why do you always have to fiddle with it?

– I don't know.

– Oh, you're such an imbecile!

I don't mean to break things. But I get a nice feeling when I look through stuff. Runa left behind so many exciting things; they're kept in a closet. When I'm home alone, I go sightseeing through the house. I try to find out who these people are. Where are they coming from and how do they live? Who are my siblings? I have a brother I know nothing about. His name is Ómar. Stebbi has a big brother who lives in his home. Gummi also has a big brother who sometimes visits him. He's an agent; he works for Customs. Anton has two brothers.

I don't really know Anton very well. I only play with him because he's so often on his own and has no one else to play with. I think he finds me annoying and stupid. He plays with me only because he doesn't know how to say no to me, or because he needs someone to kick about with. He's older than me. If we didn't live in the same neighborhood, we probably wouldn't speak.

Anton's odd. He's not like the others. But he is, too. He wears terylene pants. He has a skin disease called eximenenen. I can't say it. Sometimes Anton asks me the name of his disease.

– Eximenenen?

– What did you say?

– Eximenenen?

He thinks it's strange that I can't say it right.

The girls tease Anton by calling him Tony Terylene. This makes him really mad; he runs off to his house.

– Is Tony Terylene going home to his Mommy? they call after him.

He's very bright. He knows so much. Sometimes I'm completely confused by listening to him. Once, he told me that it would one day be the year 2000. I found that astonishing. I don't even know what year it is now.

Anton thinks I'm an idiot. He's not said so directly, but I know anyway. I can tell by the way he looks at me sometimes. His father can't stand me. He can't stand kids, but especially not me.

Once when I was asking for Anton, his father came to the door.

– Is Anton at home? I asked.

- What's it to you? he said, and shut the door.

Anton's mom is tiny and fat and definitely older than my mom; his dad is very tall and thin. Anton is often with his mom and even walks with her to the store. Sometimes they are even hand-in-hand. All the kids stop playing and start giggling when they see them walking together. There is something freaking hilarious about seeing them.

- Is that Tony Terylene out walking his dwarf?

You're a dork if you're out with your mom. I'd rather drink a bottle full of piss and eat blowflies than go to the store with my mom.

Generally, I'm not allowed over to Anton's. Everything in his room is so nice that he doesn't want me to touch anything. There's also a strange smell in his home. When I ask for him, we go out to play; I'm only allowed into the living room.

Still, I know his brothers better than my brother.

I also have a sister named Kristín. She lives in Norway. I don't know what she looks like. When she calls, Dad speaks tremendously loudly on the phone. He asks her what the weather is like in Trondheim and tells her about the weather in Iceland. When Mom talks to her, she asks what's happening and how everyone is.

Dad isn't bothered about how people are, just whether it's good weather in Trondheim, and making sure everyone there knows the weather here. When guests come to visit, he tells them about it loudly, like it's something everyone has been waiting for:

- It was cold in Trondheim last weekend!

Dad thinks Norway is the most remarkable country in the world. If someone comes to visit who has just returned from overseas and is trying to tell stories about the trip, Dad tops all their stories with some fact or other about Norway and starts telling stories about his trip to Norway. Nowhere has such good weather, such interesting buildings, or such spectacular scenery as Norway. If people try to talk about other countries, Dad drowns it out with Norway. He thinks it's pointless to travel to other countries. He doesn't think much of people who head off to Denmark.

- Did you have a good time? asks Mom.

- It was awesome.

- What was so special about it? asks Dad.

- How was the weather?

- At least twenty the whole time.

- The temperature reached twenty-five in Trondheim yesterday, Dad announces.

- Did you meet the Queen? Mom asks jokingly.

- It will never be as hot in Copenhagen as Oslo, Dad interjects.

- How hot was it when we were there? he asks Mom.

- I don't remember, she replies, brusquely.

- We went on a tour of Kronborg Castle. It was spectacular.

- But have you ever been to the cathedral in Trondheim? Dad asks loudly.

- Er, no.

Dad shakes his head. He thinks the cathedral is the most striking building in the world. Neither the pyramids in Egypt nor the Eiffel Tower in Paris are half as good as the cathedral in Trondheim. Anyone who has not been there has not seen anything.

He begins to tell the story of when he was in Norway. Mom sighs. We've all heard this story many times. Our guests fall silent and smile awkwardly.

I rummage through Grandma Anna's stuff very carefully. The only material evidence I had found of her existence were some pictures of an obese old woman with messy white hair. That was until I found a tape in Runa's stuff. It's the recording of a party. Runa and her girl-friends are drunk. They are listening to music and talking. You can't hear anything they're saying until, suddenly, one of the girls says loudly:

– Are you always alone?

– Huh? asks a sick, old woman.

She repeats the question, even more loudly.

– Are you always alone?!

– Yes, says the old lady.

Then the girl shouts back:

– Is everyone always mean to you?!

The old lady agrees.

– And you never get anything to eat?!

– No, says the old lady .

They all start laughing.

That's Grandma Anna they're teasing. I don't understand why Runa had her at a party.

Judging by her things, Grandma Anna was super infirm. There're all kinds of rubber hoses and medical junk and assorted syringes with plastic needles. I took one of the syringes. I use it as a water gun or a fire extinguisher for Action Man.

I'm looking for information about these people. I get my information from their possessions. I paw through stuff and examine their drawers, studying pictures and reading postcards. No one tells me anything. If I ask Mom, she has amnesia.

- How did you meet Dad?

- I don't remember; it was so long ago.

- Where was our first home?

- I already told you.

- Where was it again?

- On Skipholt.

- Where's that?

- Oh, stop pestering me.

It's like the past is hidden in a haze. It's like nobody wants to remember what happened. If I ask my dad, he usually just replies with total nonsense. It really depends on what sort of mood he's in. Sometimes he talks to me like I'm handicapped, or the way you talk to a toddler. I'm not a baby. Sometimes he just talks about something other than what I asked about. Often I've heard it before.

Sometimes he holds my hand with one of his hands and strokes my cheek with the other while he tells me some boring story about how everything was in the old days, when he was little: how poor everyone was and how everyone was always cold, especially him.

He tells me the same stories over and over. They are sad and also often sentimental. One story is about how when my dad was little, he and his brother killed flies on the windowsill. Then they went out and saw a dead bird and began to cry. He looks deep into my eyes as though the story is hiding some deep message about life.

He's often told me this story. I don't understand the moral. I think it's just a silly story. It's okay to kill flies.

I try to hide my hands behind my back so he can't reach them. It's uncomfortable when he holds me so hard. It's mean and annoying. He squeezes my hand and makes it hurt.

It seems like I'm an instrument on which he's trying to play a tragic, sad song.

The worst is when I need to ask Dad for money. Like when I need money to buy something or go to the movies. I try instead to ask Mom.

– Mom, can I have money for the movies?

– Ask your father.

Mom never has any money.

I get a knot of anxiety in my stomach and my mouth goes dry when I need to ask Dad for money. Sometimes it's okay and he just lets me have the money. If he's in a good mood. But if he is in a bad temper then it's not alright. When I approach him he stretches out his hand towards me. I give him my hand. Then he smiles gently at me. I have a strong feeling that he knows I'm going to ask him for money so I pretend to have some other reason for approaching him. Maybe he wants me to tell him that I am fond of him or some crap like that. You don't say such things to your parents. Though there are small children who do, and they get a treat in return.

Maybe he's hoping I'll ask him to tell me some old story. It's like

I'm meant to do something for him, or else he'll be bored.

It's a play. One he makes up. A play about a sad, benevolent dad and an ugly, ungrateful son.

– You want to have a conversation with your dad?

– Yes, I mumble.

– Tell me something interesting.

– Can I have some money for the movies? I say quietly.

His face falls. He wasn't expecting that. It's like I've slapped him around the face with a wet rag. He's disappointed and troubled.

First he sighs:

– Phwww.

I fall silent and look down at my feet. I know what's coming.

– Movies? Didn't I just give you money for movies?

He says "movies," not "the movies." That bothers me. But I don't say anything because I don't want to talk to him for any longer than is absolutely necessary.

– It's a different movie.

He sighs again, and looks down like he's utterly confused. I have this feeling that my theater trip is going to be over before it starts. I go to the movie theater about once a month.

After we've been silent for a short while, it's like he's been able to muster the spirit to get out his wallet.

– How much does the movie theater cost? he asks.

There's sadness in his voice. I've managed to hurt him.

I tell him the cost. He takes the money out of his wallet and puts it in my hand. Then he squeezes our palms together and smiles weakly.

I feel like I hurt him, but not enough to break him completely. He's good and gives me money even though I'm ugly and evil.

We stand like this for a moment. He won't let go of my hand; instead, he squeezes it. Again I feel like there's a stone slab lying across my chest. I can't breathe. My stomach gets all warm. I feel sick. It's like he's forcing me to eat something I don't want to. I want to scream: Stop it, it's mean! But I steel myself.

– I need bus fare as well, I mutter.

There are tears in his eyes. He shakes his head as though he is both disappointed and surprised.

– How much? he asks, determinedly.

His tone is impersonal. It's like he's talking to someone he doesn't know. Someone who is annoying and stupid. Dad definitely talks this way to criminals at work. The way he asks his question sounds like robbers have asked him for a ransom to get back a loved one, a ransom he doesn't think he can meet.

I murmur the amount, ashamed. I feel like I'm evil; I've managed to wound him grievously. He gives me the money. He doesn't take my hand. His eyes are full of sadness.

– Thanks, I mumble, trying to sound friendly.

He shrugs his shoulders.

I'm troubled when Dad is in one of these moods. It's like all his grief and everything he has seen and experienced at work floods over me and burrows deep inside.

I decide to not ask for money for candy. It's a luxury I can do without on this occasion.

Sometimes, after these encounters, it's like he realizes why I'm so tedious. It's not always this way. Sometimes he spreads out his outstretched arms, hugging me close and whispering something I don't catch but know I'm meant to agree to, some promise I'm meant to keep. Usually, it's a promise to be hardworking or not spend the money all at once.

I have to tear myself free from his arms. He lets me go slowly and whispers and mumbles all the time and strokes me on the cheek. I smile politely, nod my head and promise anything and everything.

But most of the time, all I do is manage to hurt him; he is left lonely and bored while I go to the movies to have fun with my friends.

X

I don't know what he wants from me. I think maybe he feels bad about work and doesn't have anyone to talk to. Perhaps he wants me to hug him. Or else he wants me to be more like Anton, calm and good and wearing terylene pants and accompanying him places the way Anton accompanies his mom.

I know my dad. But I don't know who he is. He knows me, but not really. He's seldom normal around me. I feel a little for him in our relationship. I think sometimes he feels there's not that much worth caring about in me. He never praises anything I do and he belittles me when no one can hear. When he feels bad, it's like he wants me to feel bad, too.

Sometimes he asks me about something I'm doing. But when I start to tell him, he stops listening to me and listens to the radio or something while I'm talking. That makes me miserable. I think he wants me to be miserable.

Everyone else thinks Dad's great. Strangers tell me how interesting he is, or how hardworking, or how fortunate I am that he is my dad. They don't know him the way he is at home. Maybe he changes as soon as he gets home. He's always happy and fun when he's out. Dad's more interesting around people he doesn't know.

Sometimes he comes out to the soccer pitch to fetch me for dinner. I try to run over to him so that the other kids won't meet him.

He doesn't say "soccer;" he says "kickball." And he calls the football a "bladder" or a "pigskin."

– Is this your bladder, Jón?

The other kids think he's funny and entertaining. But I don't want him to entertain them. I want him to entertain me.

I examine my family's clothes; I read postcards they've written or received. Kristín left a lot of CDs in plastic cases. Now and then I listen to *Fröken Fraken* by Sven Ingvars; as I listen, I try to imagine my sister. I'm no closer to her. Ómar left nothing behind. It's like the earth swallowed him. I don't remember him at all. He's a completely closed book. When he comes to visit I greet him with a handshake and introduce myself. Runa I know the most about. She's really my only sibling, at least the only one I'd recognise in the street.

Most of all, I'd like to know about my parents, these strange people who live with me but never say anything that reveals their identity. Who is Dad? What does he feel? What is Mom thinking all that time she's sitting in the kitchen? Where did they meet and why did they get married? How are they doing? How do they feel about me?

I root about in closets, scour letters, sniff clothes, pore over images, and try to puzzle together from it all a picture of the secret facets of my existence.

△

- Where are my dolls? asks Runa.

- I didn't take them.

- Yes, you did. You took them.

- No, it was Action Man.

Runa starts laughing.

- What? asks Mom from the kitchen.

- He's completely cracked, this boy. He says Action Man took my dolls.

- Just leave him be.

Sometimes I'm playing with Action Man when I come across stuff. Action Man is my friend. He's my favorite toy. I also have The Lone Ranger. He's not as cool as Action Man. He's also a cowboy. I'd have preferred Tonto because he's an Indian. The Lone Ranger does the dangerous tasks. Sometimes it lands him in a lot of trouble and he needs Action Man to save him.

Once I made a parachute out of a plastic bag and let The Lone Ranger test it. I threw him over the roof of the house.

He broke both his legs.

Then Action Man turned into a doctor. He took The Lone Ranger home and fixed his legs with scotch tape.

I'd never do that with Action Man. I take great care of him.

He was with me when I found the dolls. Two of them. One had long blond hair and the other was a brunette with short hair. I took them out of the box and went outside with them. I didn't mean to break them. It happened inadvertently. I was playing that some bad guys had taken them captive and tied them together over a fire pit. I hung them from a wooden spit using some wire, and lit the fire. Action Man had to save them. But while I was playing with him, the fire got so big it burnt the dolls.

I held a funeral for them. I dug a hole and put them in it. Then I shovelled it over and set a cross there. Action Man and The Lone Ranger were the only guests at the funeral.

I can't tell Runa what happened. She'll definitely get mad. I'd find it annoying if someone took Action Man and broke him.

I go outside. Mom and Runa are still talking in the kitchen.

Spring is in the air. The snow is gone and the sun is shining. It's only a little bit cold. I go over to Stebbi's. Stebbi is my friend. He's in the Indian Club with me. We're the only two people in it. No one else is allowed to be in our Indian Club.

◉ ■ ◿ ✗ ◢ ■ ● ☉ ◖ △ ✗

When we grow up, we're going to move to Arizona and live like real Indians in protected areas. Stebbi even has an Indian costume his mom sewed him. But he can't use it because it's too small.

I ring the bell. His mother comes to the door.

– Is Stefan home?

I take care not to call him Stebbi. If I do, his mom says that there isn't a Stebbi who lives there. She wants him to be called Stefan.

– Are you wearing your long johns? she asks.

– Yes.

I pull up my pant leg and show her. Stebbi's mother is a good woman. She's strict, but still good. She doesn't want me to get cold. Many parents don't want their kids playing with me. Some forbid it outright.

– Want to play?

– No, I can't play with you.

– Why not?

– My mom's forbidden it.

Maybe the kids are just using this as an excuse because they don't want to play with me. Most of my friends' parents have forbidden their children from playing with me at some point or other. But not Stebbi's mom. She's the only one who can read my dad's handwriting for me.

Sometimes when I come home, there's a note on the table my dad has written. I can't read his handwriting. No one in the street can read his handwriting except Stebbi's mother.

I'd never prank her. I'd never throw eggs at her door or put a water hose through her window or a dead bird in her mailbox. Or cat poop in her shoe or in the pocket of her coat.

But when I was little, I did damage her campervan. I didn't mean to. I broke all its windows and lights. I don't know why. Sometimes I do things and I don't know why I do them. I just do, not realizing what I've done until afterwards.

Stebbi comes to the door.

– Want to play?

– Play what?

– Outside somewhere.

We walk down into the valley. We're Indians. Stebbi is a riot. Though sometimes he's a bit of a coward. One time, we ran away from home and were going to sleep in an igloo. We were going to live as long as it was snowing. But Stebbi got homesick. We started to fight and he began to cry so I took him back home. And once we were going to go on an adventure. We spread peanut butter on crackers and put juice in a bottle. He was wearing his Indian costume and I had my feather headdress. We both had our knives. We were going to stay out all day and try to go somewhere no one had ever gone before. But halfway there Stebbi pooped his pants and we had to turn around.

– Shall we set something on fire?

– Do you have any matches?

I show him my matchbox. It's full.

– Wow!

When we get down into the valley we go straight into the ditch. Indians don't let anyone see them when they are sneaking about.

We pad along the bottom of the ditch through the valley. From time to time we try to light a small fire but the grass is so short that the fire dies out. We go past Fossvogs School towards the forest. No one sees us.

Along the way, we see a dead sheep that has drowned in the ditch. I poke her in the back with a stick and then turn her head up out of the black swampy water. It's a disgusting sight. She has no eyes. We hurry on.

In front of the forest is a large patch of withered grass. We hide ourselves in the trees and after a while light a fire. This fire doesn't die out; it grows quickly and spreads out. White fumes of smoke climb to the sky. Once the fire is lit in one place, we run away. We hide ourselves and see if any adults turn up. Then we light a fire somewhere else.

It's not long before the fires cover a huge area. There's a lot of smoke over the neighborhood. We look at each other, flushed, full of excitement and anticipation. We know, of course, that we're not allowed to set fires. But they're so much fun. And it's not dangerous. I don't know anyone who's died from a grass fire. They light one in

Fossvogur every spring. What kids think is fun often gets banned. And adults think things are incredibly dangerous when they aren't.

- Shouldn't we stop now? asks Stebbi.

- Hold on, I say.

I tear up a large bunch of withered grass and set fire to it. Then I run around and set fires wherever there isn't a fire. Stebbi is obviously stressed out.

- Be careful!

The smoke gets in my eyes and blinds me. The heat is unbearable; I can't breathe. There's fire everywhere! I feel a chilling sting on one leg and look down. My pants are on fire. I smack the fire with my palms and it goes out. My leg is scorched and smarting. But my fear gets the better of my pain. What have I done?

- Jónsi?

I can't think. I run towards the voice. The smoke is so thick that I can't see anything. I don't see Stebbi until I am almost on top of him.

- Wow!

- Are you crazy?!

His voice shivers with fear. I can hear the lump welling in his throat. We run away. Behind us rises an ocean of fire, like a giant wall is crossing the valley, pushing the smoke ahead of it.

We run into the forest and throw ourselves down in the shade of a large tree. I check my pants. There's a fist-sized hole burned into the bottom of one leg. The skin of the leg is red and swollen and it's really singed.

- Are you hurt?

- Yes, I say.

Actually, nothing hurts. Just a tiny sting. Indians never feel pain. They can run if they have a broken foot and shoot a bow if both their hands are broken. No matter how much you torture them, they never tell. I make it look like I'm feeling great, but I'm not doing so well.

– I looked down and my whole leg was on fire! I report.

– You burned your hair, too.

I don't believe that! Stebbi points and I feel my hair. It's singed in places! Mom won't be happy. I get tears in my eyes at the thought. Mom's going to find out it was me who set the fires in the area. She's going to majorly scold me. Instantly my daring thoughts turn into a paralyzing fear. No Indian is so strong that he is unafraid of his mother. I can't take it, and I start crying.

We wriggle to our feet and run out of the forest. We look carefully around us before we climb over the fence. We jump up onto the pavement and walk casually home. No one seeing us could suspect that we'd been setting fires. We look like two really good boys coming from visiting their grandmother. I even feign surprise at the smoke, and we look at it, shocked, like we don't understand how people can get up to such mischief.

Suddenly, the screeching sound of brakes, a splitting siren. Two fire engines zoom past at top speed with lights flashing, an ambulance immediately on their heels. We hurry after them. This we don't want to miss. Moments later, the cops come by. The blood in my veins freezes. We're going to be arrested. We might even go to jail. I want to run and hide in a nearby yard. But I can't move. My lower lip starts quivering uncontrollably. The incriminating evidence is all over me. I'm literally red-handed. I'm ready to confess everything and try to escape with a promise never to do it again. Never! But the police have no interest in us; they drive past at full speed.

– We ought to go home.

- Hold on.

- Jónsi!

- I want to see. Come on.

We edge nearer to the cars. What an exciting spectacle! Everything has been upended. Cops and firefighters wearing yellow rubber clothes are running about. The fire is unbelievably large. I feel a humble pride that this was our handiwork. The firefighters are spraying the fire with a really powerful hose. No one notices us or stops us. On one fire truck, there's a box full of special rakes. The men are beating the flaming grass with them. I make a decision. Without saying a word, I grab a rake and go out onto the burning battlefield. I smack the fire like my life depends on it. A warlike fireman nods his head, pleased with me. I call to a guy with a hose and point out a flaming tussock.

- It's over here, too!

They direct the hose there. I run under the jet, unafraid, and smack the fire down with a rake. Then I give the signal that everything is okay. They direct the hose elsewhere. Stebbi watches me, his eyes full of admiration. I'm a hero. I'm fearless in the face of fire. And I was almost burned to death. I'm going to be a fireman when I grow up. I'm going to save people and go to school and teach kids not to tamper with fire. I hammer and smack the rake alongside the firemen until the whole fire is put out.

By this time, a lot of people are watching. Nobody, though, dares to help out. I've got wet through and am soot-black up to my head. I walk over to Stebbi.

- Well, now we're done, I report, smugly.

A heavy hand is on my shoulder. I feel a surge of panic when I look up and see a big cop and another, still larger, behind him.

I think maybe someone saw us light the fires and told the police. I try to make my features as surprised and innocent as I can.

- Hey, you kids, says the policeman.

I can feel my heart beat ever faster. I'm going to be put in cuffs. In my mind, I make up fake stories about our day. If someone saw us in the valley, then I'm going to say we were headed to see pigs on a farm, for a school project. Then they'll think we are well-behaved boys who are always learning, the sort of boys who don't set fires.

If no one saw us, then we were going to visit a disabled boy, the brother of a boy in our class. In that case, we're also very good.

But an alibi proves unnecessary.

- You're helpful boys, says the cop.

I breathe easy. No one suspects us of mischief. We're heroes. The firemen come over and congratulate us. One pats me on the head in a friendly way.

- Yes, if only all boys were so conscientious.

- Did you see who started the fire? asks the cop.

I'm right in with a response. It's my standard reply in these situations, something I always tell an adult if they suspect I've broken something. It comes in handy a lot. It's one hundred percent convincing.

- It was some teenagers, I think. At least, I saw them running away.

It's good to blame teenagers because adults always think they're up to no good. Teenagers are also really annoying. Everyone thinks so.

The cop nods. He's completely sold.

- Can I get a picture of you with the boys?

It's a photographer from one of the newspapers.

- Say cheese!

We pose with the officers and firemen. He takes a picture.

- Magic, he says.

After endless thanks and praise, the police take us home. The policeman goes with me to the front door.

Mom's face falls when she sees me.

- What have you done now?
- I just helped some firemen put out a small fire.

The policeman backs up my story, telling my mother how lucky she is to have such a thoughtful and hard-working boy and how I helped them extinguish the fire.

- Some teenagers started it, I say.

I can see Mom isn't completely convinced. She never believes me. It's like she can tell when I'm lying. But my story isn't wholly untrue. I did help them put out the fire.

I take a bath. Mom cleans my hair and cuts off the burned parts. I don't say anything. She doesn't, either. She's decided not to ask me anything. She's aware it pays to know as little as possible. Yet I know what she knows: that it was me who started the fire. I try to find something to say, but nothing comes to mind.

The next day, there's a picture of me and Stebbi on the back of the *Daily News* under the headline WILDFIRE IN FOSSVOGUR. The article says that the fire department only just managed to save the forest from being completely burned to the ground. There was significant damage to trees that had recently been planted. And the neighboring houses had been at great risk from the fire. Several were evacuated due to the danger; one person had to go to the hospital because of smoke inhalation. Under the picture of me and Stebbi, it said: "Two boys who helped put out the fire."

I don't show my mother the picture.

◉

[…] He seems very distant in his character; his
social inclination is far behind what is expected
for his age group. The boy seems unable to consider
the consequences of his actions, and is only able
to make weak and futile attempts to bring some
structure to his thoughts and his world. If the
boy's environment is not to blame, I strongly
suspect he is brain damaged.

(National Hospital, Psychiatric Ward,
Children's Hospital Trust, 07/03/1977)

✕

I creep along the hallway. No one hears a thing. I open the kitchen cabinet gently and take out a roll of butcher's string. Mom uses this string to stitch together Icelandic haggis. I tear off a decent length and put the butcher's string back in the cupboard.

I sneak back along the corridor. I place Mom's slippers on either side of the corridor. I put them on their ends up against the wall, heels in the air. Then I stretch the string tightly between them. After that, I go back into the kitchen and hide myself under the kitchen table.

A little time passes, then Grandma Guðrún comes along. She's dressed in a light bathrobe with gray overalls on top of it. She's wearing thick tights, and slippers. She's also in black men's socks, like the ones my dad wears.

It's funny to see such an old woman in Dad's socks.

Grandma Guðrún is blind. Her eyes are open and work normally, but she simply doesn't see anything through them. When she walks, she doesn't lift her legs like normal people: she slides them across the floor, gently stroking the surface with her soles to test what's in front of her.

She starts walking along the hallway. She uses her hands to help feel her way. I manage to contain my laughter. She runs her feet into the string. She doesn't cotton on immediately, not until the shoes have fallen over and are dragging after her. Then she bends down and investigates what's happening.

- What's this here?

I burst out laughing. It's a very funny sight. Grandma smiles benignly.

- Well, now, is that you, little Jón? Get on with you!

She frees the string from her legs and heads into the bathroom.

Grandma's old. She's more than 90 years old. She was born in the year seventeen hundred and sour cabbage. Her face is all puckered and she's got white hair. She lives with us, in the room next to mine.

Grandma looks after me during the day when Mom is working. She sits in her room all day and knits and listens to the radio. She doesn't pay me any mind. She only comes out to get herself coffee.

When Runa moved out, Grandma got her room. Runa has a boyfriend and lives with him. He's called Grétar. He's really tough; he listens to the Rolling Stones. All the boys in the street agree that he's the toughest guy they've ever seen. He's much cooler than Anton's brother and even cooler than Gummi's brother, even though Gummi's brother owns a Jeep, a Lada Sport.

Grétar doesn't need a Jeep. He's got long hair. He's fun and likes talking to me. And he's puked up on Dad. It was after they'd been out dancing. Dad picked up Runa and Grétar because they were too drunk to drive.

When they got home, Grétar leaned towards him to thank him but instead puked all over his shoulder. Dad didn't say anything but "Goodnight" and then strolled in with vomit on his shoulder.

Runa and Grétar rolled about laughing. I would laugh too if I saw that. I would never dare puke over Dad.

Runa's trying to have a baby.

Grandma has glaucoma. There's a cloud over her eyes. But she still can tell the difference between night and day. If it's bright, she sees people as shadows. And she hears remarkably well. She always thinks there's someone with me. But there never is. I'm always playing by myself. I speak for Action Man and for the tin soldiers.

Grandma can do most things other people can, by using her hands and fingertips instead of her eyes. She dresses herself. She knows her clothes by feeling them.

And on the phone there's an extra dial on top of the standard one. The extra dial has big, raised numbers so she can make phone calls.

I like teasing Grandma. She never gets mad at me, not even when I tricked her into smelling baker's ammonia, like Runa once did to me. Sometimes I hide inside her closet and attack her when she walks past. She has an incredibly strong grip given how old she is. I think she must be the strongest old crone in Iceland.

I reach for her neck. She grabs my hands and holds me tight.

– Think you can take me on? she says.

I start laughing and run away.

There's some tape in one of the drawers that's sticky on both sides. I once put it under her slippers. When she walked, the shoes kept sticking to the floor and she had to keep tugging her legs along. I don't know what was funnier, the expression on Grandma or the sound she made when she tugged up the shoes. I rolled around laughing.

In the morning, my mom leaves coffee in a Thermos for Grandma. She puts her finger down into the cup as she pours. That's how she can tell the cup is getting full. Then, when she pours milk, she keeps her finger inside the cup, and pours milk over it to work out how much milk she's got.

Once, I put laundry detergent in her coffee. She sipped it and immediately spat it back in the cup.

– There's something not right with this coffee, little Jón. I wonder, have you done something to it?

I started cackling. She wasn't angry. We were just playing around. Grandma is fun. She gives me candy and sometimes money.

If I have money, I'll go to a kiosk and buy Bazooka chewing gum or a can of fizzy drink. There's a cartoon inside Bazooka chewing gum. It's about a boy named Bazooka Joe. I don't understand it. But it's still fun to collect the episodes. I also collect soccer cards though I'm not bothered about soccer. The soccer cards have a good smell.

I don't know which soccer players are the best. I know that Kevin Keegan is good. My favorite picture is still the one of the guy who is sitting on his haunches smiling happily, but his balls are hanging down one leg of his shorts. I crack up when I see it.

Sometimes my mom sends me to the convenience store to buy her cigarettes. I'm allowed to spend the change. Once, there were fifty cents left, so I rang home to ask my mom if I could spend it all. She said yes, but it didn't matter because it cost me fifty cents to make the call. I can be a real idiot.

I enjoy being around Grandma. I'm usually at school or outside playing during the day. I spend the evenings with Grandma. Especially when Mom and Dad are playing bridge. She kisses me good night and says the Our Father with me before I go to sleep. She bows over my chest and makes the sign of the cross. It's comforting. Grandma never goes outside. At most, she sits on the balcony in nice weather.

I can only remember one time that Grandma's been outside. It was when we were building the garage. I was playing on it. I was going to take a running start and jump over the ditch. I took a step back and fell backwards, right off the garage roof. I landed on the asphalt drive and made a hole in my head. I'd managed to turn myself a bit in the air so I could put my hands out. If I'd landed on my back, I would definitely have fractured my skull.

At first, I didn't dare move. I'd definitely broken some bones. And I was in shock.

All the kids came over, and so did some grown-ups who'd seen it happen. They all stood around me in a circle.

There wasn't much the matter. I had a wound in my head, between my eyes, and I'd scraped the skin on my palms. Nothing else. But it was fun to lie there and be the center of attention and see everyone be really concerned about me. They were talking about calling an ambulance, and someone said that I wasn't allowed to move.

Then Grandma came out. Someone had run to my house to let them know what had happened. Mom and Dad were both at work.

It was such a weird sight that everyone forgot me and just stared at her. There was a deathly silence. No one knew who she was. She was tiny, with her wild, white hair. She was in a traditional *peysufot* and slippers. It was like she'd arrived from the past by time machine and somehow landed in Fossvogur.

Her blindness made her all the stranger. She padded forward hesitantly, groping her way. If you didn't know she was blind, you'd simply think that she was distracted, or simply old and confused. If she'd been able to see, she'd have seen me surrounded by all these people.

She came our way. When she was almost on top of us, she turned her back to us and it was like she was just looking into the garden. No one said a word.

– Jón, my dear, is everything okay? she said, quietly.

It was so funny I forgot I had a wound in my head and wasn't meant to move. I forgot all about my shock. I got up and walked over to her.

– I'm right here, Grandma.

– Are you okay?

– Yes, I just have a wound in my head.

– That's good, my dear.

She held on to my elbow and I went back inside with her. We called Dad and he came and took me to the emergency room.

When I don't have any one to play with, and don't want to play on my own, I sometimes go into Grandma's room and talk to her. She tells me amusing stories about the old days. When Grandma was little, people lived in houses made of turf. There was no television or radio. There were no cars. There wasn't even electricity. Everyone was very poor and had to work hard. People were always dying because there were no doctors to cure them. Children died a lot. Sometimes two children were baptized after the same person so that the name would survive if one of the children died. It would be like if my brother's name wasn't actually Ómar but Jón, the name I got from Grandpa.

When Grandma was little, everyone had lice. At night people sat around, picking off lice and chatting.

Grandma and her friends often played at picking lice from people who were asleep. They competed to see who could find the most.

I myself have gotten lice. There was a lice outbreak in Fossvogs School because there are so many lice-rats at school who come from Blesugróf. All the kids had a note home. Mom had to delouse my hair and wash it with special lice soap. But in the old days there wasn't any lice soap. There wasn't any soap, period. Back then, people washed their hair with *keytu*, which is old piss. I don't think anyone would do that today.

Grandma also knows fairy tales. She sometimes tells me stories: the one about Búkollu the cow or the one about the idiot brothers Gísli, Eiríkur, and Helgi. In fairy tales, people have strange names and there are also trolls and elves.

Grandma has seen elves. Once, she saw a troll on the mountain above her farm. Trolls only move about at night. If the sun catches them, they turn to stone, so they have to hide deep inside their cave during the day.

Once when grandmother sat watching the sheep, she saw a female elf standing on one side of a large rock. When Grandma crept closer, she saw the elf was folding baby clothes. When the elfwoman spotted her, she hastily snatched up the clothes, walked straight into the stone, and disappeared.

- Was there a door on the stone?
- No, nothing like that.
- Why did she go inside the stone?
- The elves live in the rocks, and climb on them as they please.
- Wow!

I've never seen elves or fairies. I've not even seen a ghost. I've tried spying on the elves at the large elf stone along the road on Álfhólsvegur. I lay there waiting for hours but didn't see anything.

– They don't want to be seen, said Grandma.

– Why not?

– They fear we humans.

I can understand that. They would definitely be forced to do lots of things they wouldn't want to, like going to school. If I were an elf or a troll, I wouldn't want to draw attention to myself; I'd simply make sure to hide so I could live in peace.

Grandma never looks forward to anything.

– Aren't you looking forward to your birthday?

– No.

– Why not?

– I've had so many birthdays.

– Don't you look forward to Christmas?

– No, she says, and laughs like it's absurd to look forward to Christmas.

– Don't you love getting presents?

– No, she says, and smiles.

Amazing. I look forward to birthdays. But I look forward to Christmas even more. I look forward to it so much that I can't sleep for several nights before Christmas.

I wake up early on Christmas Eve. It's like the clock ticks slower than normal; time promises it won't ever pass. Christmas Eve lasts for several days. I look at the clock and it says two o'clock. I think many hours have gone by, I look back at it, and it's only quarter past two.

– You must look forward to something, Grandma?

– I look forward to dying.

– Why?

- I look forward to meeting my blessed Savior.

Sometimes Grandma talks about boring things. And she describes them as though I've never heard of them before. They are always the same stories, mostly about people who died. They're sentimental and Grandma gets sad when she tells them. She becomes like my dad.

The one about Vigdís from Muli's deathbed is especially annoying. It's about a woman who was very ill for a long time; she was in a lot of torment before she died.

- Her face was disfigured by the pain...her little boy sat at her bedside, and she held his little hand...

I don't bother listening to that stupid story.

- Her chest rattled as though each breath was going to be her last.

I go get myself some Cocoa Puffs. Grandma doesn't eat Cocoa Puffs. She thinks they taste bad. She thinks that about Coke, too.

- Pff! It's just mud and sugar.

And she's never watched television. It wasn't invented until after she became blind.

Poor grandmother.

There's a strange lamp on the table. The shade rotates when you turn on the light and you can see all kinds of landscapes on it. It's almost like the movies. It says MALLORCA on the side.

Gummi's been to Mallorca. He went there with his mom and dad. He was totally tanned when he came back. You could really tell because he is so blond.

I liked seeing the pictures from Mallorca. Gummi had a folder full of them: of the beach, the zoo, and other places. In one picture, he's holding an enormous parrot, like Kiki in Enid Blyton's *The Adventure Series*. That's pretty cool. On the wall of his room there's a poster with a picture of him on it. The poster reads: WANTED. Under the image is written: REWARD $50,000. Total fake.

I went abroad, once. I went to Denmark and Norway with Mom and Dad. I went to Tívoli and the zoo, but there aren't any pictures.

There aren't many pictures of me at home. In one photo, I'm standing with my parents but you can't see my face because I'm reading *Duck Tales*. There's a picture of me when I was little; it hangs on the wall inside the television room. There's also one of Grandma Anna holding me. I haven't seen many pictures of her, either. Mom and Dad never take pictures of me. The only nice picture I've got of myself is a picture Gummi took with his camera, when it was my birthday.

In Denmark, I went to childcare with some strangers. That was fun. We went out into the woods and hunted frogs. After that, I went with my parents to Norway to visit my sister Kristín.

I'd like to have a photo album full of pictures of myself. I'd be able to look at them and recall all the good memories. I could show them to my friends and tell stories about what happened.

Many things at Gummi's house have Mallorca written on them: ashtrays and wall plates. Inside the living room, on a high-up shelf, there's a huge, black bull with horns. It says TORRES on it. His parents bought it when they were in Mallorca.

When Gummi got back from Mallorca he gave me a saltcellar and a little pirate pistol with caps. You can only shoot one shot at a time. But it shoots brilliantly.

Gummi is my friend. He's always kind to me. He never fights with me and doesn't make fun of me when I do weird things. His mom and dad are always nice to me, too.

I always invite Gummi to my birthdays and he usually invites me to his. It was his birthday the first time I ever went to his house. He'd just moved into the neighborhood. I didn't have anyone to play with that day. I knew a boy had recently moved in to that house so I went and asked for him. His mother answered the door.

- Is there a boy here?

She let me in. There was a birthday party going on. I got cookies and soda. After that, we were friends.

I sometimes pull pranks. I like to tease annoying people. I tease this one guy who lives in the street next to Gummi. He's always annoying us kids. If our ball goes into his garden, he always takes it, and we can't get our ball back. So many balls disappear. So I peed in a punctured ball. Then I went and kicked another ball several times at the wall of his house. I knew it would get on his nerves a lot.

After I'd been kicking the ball against his house a while, I took the pee-ball and threw it in his garden.

He came right out.

- Can I have my ball?

- No, you're never getting it back.

- You're annoying and you stink!

When he picked up the ball, it sprayed pee all over him. I started laughing and ran off. A few times, I've thrown stink bombs into his garden.

I also like to tease Posh Friðjón. He lives in our street, too. He's not annoying. He's always friendly to kids. All he ever does is sweep and tidy the outside of his house. Sometimes he sweeps the sidewalk in the street. He's even swept the road once or twice. He wants everything to be neat. That's why it's so much fun to tease him. Like I've thrown sand on the pavement next to him. I've thrown mud at his door. Once Gummi and I stole some eggs from Mom and threw them at his windows and front door.

I also sometimes ring and run, or pack snowballs into exhaust pipes. It's perfectly harmless; all boys do it.

But some of the things I do are a total surprise. They're things I wasn't planning to do. I don't know why I do them. They happen inadvertently. Once, for example, I was playing with my Matchbox cars in the basement. There was a large windowpane standing against the wall; Dad was going to put it in the living room. One of my cars accidentally went behind the window and I couldn't get to it. So I took an empty bottle and broke the window so I could fetch the car. I didn't mean to ruin it. It wasn't planned. Dad went crazy and spanked me.

People often get angry at me. Sometimes I know why; usually I don't. They often don't realize that what I did wasn't intentional.

Every New Year's Eve we visit my aunt and uncle. They live in an apartment building in Breiðholt. We eat a meal with them, watch the Billy Smart Circus, and set off fireworks.

They have a lot of kids and know how to make real fries. Mom just makes artificial ones. When we have chicken for dinner, we have fries from a can. They're thin and hard.

Once, when we were going home, I was a little way in front of Mom and Dad. My cousins were up on the balcony with sparklers. I was waving goodbye to them. So they could see me better, I climbed up on the roof of a car. The old man who owned the car came running. He was totally furious. He shook me all over and yelled at me. I was so scared I started crying.

Mom was upset, not at me but at the guy. That was nice of her. It was quite a surprise. I hadn't spoiled anything, just waved goodbye.

When I do something inadvertently I often feel bad afterwards because I don't know why I did it in the first place. Maybe I'm just evil. Maybe there is one Jón who is good and another Jón who is evil who makes the good Jón get up to all sorts of mischief. Maybe Satan's gotten inside me.

I often play in construction sites. I know it's forbidden but it's so much fun. It's like being in a fort. You've got to be careful not to step on a board full of nails, though. That mega sucks. I've stepped on a nail stick several times. Once, Gummi and I were playing, and Gummi trod so hard on a nail that the nail went right through his foot: the tip came up out of his instep. Gummi started bawling and had to go to the emergency room.

Once, I climbed up on the roof of a ranch house that was being built. There was scaffolding around the whole thing. When I was up on the roof, I realized that there were people working on the house: I saw their heads peeping up from the roof's edge. They'd left their tools up on the roof.

It was a game of cowboys and Indians. I was an Indian out stalking. They were the cowboys. I crawled along the roof and took a hammer. The men hadn't spotted me. I hit one of them on the head with a hammer. It wasn't hard, there was no blood or anything, but he was still really, really mad. I was so scared that I ran away and jumped off the roof.

I don't know why I do these random things. I just suddenly start doing them. My dad asks me why. I don't know what to say.

– Why did you do it? he asks.

He's angry.

– I don't know, I mumble. It's all I can say.

– Exactly: you never know anything!

It's true. I hardly know a thing. I don't want to learn or to have friends. I don't behave myself. That's why I can never go fishing with my dad or on his trips when he goes out west. You can't take me anywhere.

X

- Want to play a game? asks Gummi.

  - What game?

Gummi has lots of games. He's so grown-up and calm and knows so much. He's got everything ordered and tidy in his room and keeps it all that way. My room's just piles of junk.

Gummi has a gift for making models and painting them. He has a lot of cars and planes that he built himself. I thought it would be shit easy so I bought a model plane at The Play House. I never managed to get it together. The result was ugly, nothing like the picture on the box. I had glue all over my hands and there were also large blobs of glue all over the model. It was a Spitfire. I stuffed it with cotton and gasoline, set light to it and threw it off the roof.

  - Memory?

That's no fun. You have to remember images. I can't remember anything and I always confuse the images. It's annoying, like Mastermind. That's the most annoying game I know.

  - Let's play Monopoly.

  - Okay.

Monopoly is a great game. I like playing board games with dice and money. I love saving money and having a lot of it. Though Risk is my absolute favorite. It takes a really long time to play. I play it by myself. I've made my own maps using big drawing sheets I got from school. They're half the size of the board that comes with the game.

I drew new countries and colored them with markers. I created new rules and new cards. In my Risk, there's money. I use money from the Fisheries game. You get a certain amount of money for each country you control. And you can also sell troops. With the money, you can buy cannons that can go over land, or else ships. They can only be used once and are more expensive if you are sailing a long way. If you've got a whole ton of money, you can even buy a nuclear bomb. Those kill an entire country including everyone inside it.

I like to build a large army. When I have a much larger army than all the others, I take them on all of a sudden and kill them in a flash offensive, sailing with all my ships and bombing the biggest countries with my nuclear bomb.

I play by myself a lot, both Risk and the Fisheries game. That can last infinitely because I control the bank and can create new money. The bank lends to anyone who doesn't have any money.

I like playing alone. No one interferes and stops things or is a sore loser. I sometimes lie awake the whole night playing by myself. Each game can take many days. Sometimes I win. But I lose a lot, too.

I mostly play indoor games in the winter. In spring, outdoor games start. There's also no school. And during the summer I'm not really ever at home. I go out in the morning and come home for dinner. There's no one at home except Grandma Guðrún. She'd rather just sit in her room, knitting and listening to the radio. My mom works in the cafeteria in the City Hospital. She makes food for the patients. She usually comes home with food for me in plastic boxes. Sometimes she has fruit cocktail and I get it for dessert.

If I go on a day trip, Mom makes me lunch. She puts milk or juice in a bottle and makes me a cheese sandwich with rye bread and

French bread. I like mixing them.

Usually I go up to Big Forest. It's not far away, close to Bústaða Church.

If Stebbi's with me, we play cowboys and Indians or hold a meeting of the Indian Club. If Kristján Þór is with me, we play all kinds of games. But if I'm alone, I just mess about, throwing my knife at trees or spying on people who walk past going through the woods.

Sometimes people come into the forest to have a fight. It's very exciting to sneak up close to them and hear what they are saying. Sometimes people kiss. Once, a grown man and a woman were cuddling up against a tree. They didn't say anything; they just made cuddling noises. I was right next to them, behind the man. The woman didn't see me because she had her eyes closed. I think they were getting laid. They kissed and he kept pushing her against the tree, again and again. I wanted to leap out at them or make fun of them somehow, but I didn't dare.

I also sometimes go to Öskjuhlíð. It's fun there. But it's a long walk and it sucks if it starts raining. I usually only go when it's really great weather. There's a forest. The best thing is playing in the plane the Fire Department uses for practice. You can go inside. It's totally burned up but it still has seats and a cockpit. If you walk towards the back, the tail falls down with a heavy thud. Then if you run towards the cockpit, the nose falls down and slams into the ground so you get flung forward.

On Öskjuhlíð, there are all kinds of tunnels and bunkers the British military left behind. After the war, my parents lived in the old barracks huts on Skólavörðuholt, where Hallgrím's Church is now. They shared a Nissen hut with another couple. My brother Ómar grew up in the hut.

There were no radiators; the hut was heated by a single stove in the center of the room.

Mom sometimes tells stories about this period. My favorite story takes place at Christmas. Mom and the other woman had cleaned the whole hut from floor to ceiling. Then, while Mom was in town, my dad came home with firewood: he'd found an old telephone pole.

The pole was so long that he just put one end into the stove. When Mom came back, Dad was sitting like he was hypnotized, staring into the fire. The pole had been treated with tar and the stove was open: black soot now covered the hut Mom had just cleaned.

– What the hell have you been doing? Mom shouted.

Dad didn't notice anything; he simply stared at the fire.

– Remarkable how the stones explode in the heat, he muttered.

It's a funny story. I think Dad's great in it. I want to be like that when I grow up. There's lots I want to do with my dad. I wish he felt I was interesting and wanted to be around me and didn't find me annoying.

Once, I was home alone with Dad when Mom went to London. We were watching TV and I asked Dad to make popcorn. The popcorn was so disgustingly salty; it was inedible. Dad thought it was fine. But I couldn't eat it. He left the room again and I followed him. He was fixing the popcorn by putting sugar in it so the taste of the salt would disappear. I tasted the popcorn but it was even more yucky than before, salty and sweet. So he rinsed it under water and tried to wash the salt and sugar off, but the popcorn just became wet crap that we had to throw out. My dad was really astonished.

I thought that was great. That time, Dad was fun. I'm sure he's like that at work, all the time.

Once, Mom told him to make meat soup. She told him what to put in it. Dad put everything together in a saucepan. He remembered her telling him that he should put cornflakes in, too, so he put the whole package of cornflakes in the pot and then the soup became some kind of cornflake porridge with meat and rutabaga.

– What got into your mind?

– Didn't you tell me to put these in?

– Cornflakes? Does that even make sense?

Dad tasted the soup-porridge.

– I think it tastes good!

I wish my dad was like this more often, and allowed me to spend time with him.

It's fun when Dad's in a good mood. That's when he's being himself, not just pretending. It makes me feel loved. I hate it when he's bullshitting me or twisting what I say and trying to mock me.

During the summer, Kristján Þór and I sometimes go down to Elliðaár River. I've been going there since I was little. I almost drowned once when I fell into the river. There was a man who saved me.

We fish for salmon under the bridge. It's easy. We arrange a line of rocks in a circle in the water by the bank and trap the fish inside. Then we reach them by grabbing them and throwing them on the land. One time, a man came from the paper and took a picture of us. The news in the paper said that no one fished in the Elliðaár except for two resourceful boys.

I was very proud of this. Dad cut out the article and boasted about it to a guy in the street. He said that I'd inherited his fishing skills. He was proud of me and that felt good.

When I was little, I once cycled all the way down to the harbor and caught scorpion fish. At the time I had a blue Velamos bike; later, I got a Chopper. I put the scorpion fish in a bag and took them home and gave them to Mom.

– I hunted us some dinner, I announced.

Mom took the scorpion fish and threw them in the trash without me seeing. Then she took some haddock out of the freezer and boiled it instead, but she told me it was scorpion fish. She only told me the truth later. I ate the fish with the best appetite. The tastiest scorpion fish I ever ate.

I've heard that fish tastes best if you have caught it yourself. Mom tells the story sometimes and we laugh about it together. I like it when I do things Mom enjoys. So much of the time I'm simply an annoyance.

When we're done playing, we get milk and cookies from Gummi's mom.

- How's your mother?

- Good, I reply.

Mom and Dad are different from other parents. They're old. They're often tired and need to rest. They are often tired of me. I can be a challenge. Other kids' parents never take naps. But I'm not like other kids. Perhaps they always need to take naps because I'm so weird.

After dinner, all the kids meet at the parking spots and play dodgeball. That's fun. All the kids are playing together. It's easy to play dodgeball. It's not nearly as complicated as soccer. I'm bored by soccer. When the kids play soccer, they'd prefer it I wasn't allowed to take part. That's just as boring. It's better to be included than excluded. I have to stand and watch and I don't know what to do.

- Can I join in now?

- No, in a minute...

When I'm sick of waiting I puke on the soccer pitch. I can honestly puke when I want. I learned how to do that when I was practicing burping and talking at the same time. It's fun to talk while burping. I just contract my stomach and belch, and then the food comes up and I have complete control over it. When they leave me out too long I pull this trick and I vomit on the pitch so they can't play.

- Yuck! Man, you're disgusting!

After that, we start doing something else that I'm allowed to do.

When a lot of time has passed, Mom comes out onto the sidewalk and calls me home.

The other kids are beginning to drift off home, too.

I brush my teeth and kiss Grandma good night. I go to my room. But I don't go to sleep immediately. I play Fisheries for a bit. I crawl into bed and read. I read a book about Paddington that I took out from the library. I can't stop reading until it's over. Only then can I go to sleep. I close my eyes and imagine I'm in a strange city. I often do that.

I'm standing on the street. There's no one there, even though there usually is.

I know this neighborhood. If you go left, you come to the big house with many rooms and lots of windows facing the street. No one lives in the house.

You can go up some stairs that lead all the way up to the roof. On the roof there's all kinds of shit, like it's a rubbish dump. I sometimes lie on the roof, throwing stones at the soldiers walking past below. I have to take care they don't shoot me.

If you go right, you come to a big palace. There are stairs leading up to it. When you enter, you see two large rooms downstairs. They're empty. That's because no one lives in the palace.

From the entrance, two stairways lead to the upper floor. They're curved. They're to either side of the entrance but they curve together by the time you reach the upper floor. It doesn't matter which set of stairs you choose: they end up in the same place.

On the upper floor there's nothing but a balcony facing out to the street.

Behind the right-hand stairs, on the ground floor, is a secret door made of the same wood as the stairs. It's not visible; you have to know about it to be able to open the door. Through it, a passage goes under the road and into the big house. It ends inside a wardrobe in one of the rooms.

The only way out of the neighborhood is at the end of the street. There's a tall fence. First, you need to go past three automatic guns. They're buried in the ground. You can't see them, except for the convex cover over them. If someone chances to come close, they spring up from the ground and shoot them.

I have to be careful. Sometimes there are lions and polar bears in the neighborhood. They hide in one of the rooms of the house or in the shadows where they aren't visible.

I run into the house. There are two polar bears in the hallway. As soon as they see me they come running towards me. I turn around and run across the street and into the palace. They follow me. I go through the secret door and into the tunnel. I heave a sigh of relief. I hear them scrape and growl outside the door. They smell me. I run off.

I open the closet carefully. There's no one in the room. I sneak out of it and close it quietly behind me. Lions hear so well. At the least sound, they come running.

I look out of the window and across the street. Polar bears are still looking for me in the hall.

There is no one in the corridor. I run to the stairs and up them. Once I'm up high, the lions come for me. They scream and start chasing me up the stairs. But they can't reach me; I've come so high.

Finally I come to the roof. I lock the roof door, which is made of iron. Here, I'm safe. Wild animals can't get up here, nor the soldiers. I relax and fall asleep..

△

- There's a fight today after school!

This is wonderful news.

- Kúrland and Kjalarland against Hörðaland and Hulduland.

Street battles are a regular occurrence in Fossvogur. They're fought with swords and shields. Crazy kids clash with each other. You're not allowed any iron weapons. One time, a boy got hit in the head with an iron pipe and got a concussion.

The sides are divided by streets. I have friends on Hörðaland and Hulduland. But friendships don't exist during a street fight.

I run home right after school to prepare myself.

I stop at a construction site on the way and find some material for a sword. I choose a long, thick plank.

Some of the kids have a cool sword and even a shield with a picture on it. Gummi's dad helped him make a shield. It's large and triangular with a black eagle on the front. Behind it there's a handle made of a leather strap. Gummi also has a super sword.

Dad doesn't know anything about carpentry and doesn't have time to help me. I'd like a real sword, something that doesn't break right away when you start fencing with it.

I wind string around the end of the wood and cover it with duct tape. That's my handle. I saw a little stump off the end, and put it crossways. That's the hilt which protects your hand from getting hit. I fasten it carefully by covering it with duct tape. I know that it's not a good idea to hammer nails into such a narrow piece of wood. First, there's nothing for them to hold on to, and second, the wood splits easily. Tape is much better.

My plank is longer than most swords. That makes it a better weapon. But stabbing and thrusting gets more tiring quicker with a long sword rather than a short blade.

It doesn't mean anything to be stabbed by a sword. It's not the same rules as war. You aren't dead, not even if you get stabbed. You have to give up, instead.

It's different in shoot and run or cops and robbers. Then if you shoot someone he's dead. Though some kids never admit they're dead.

You have to be well prepared. Fossvogur is full of all kinds of gangs, many of which I don't know. Street fights can be dangerous.

The teen gangs are from Grímsbær. Grímsbær gangs are dangerous. They own a motorcycle and they punch. They take captives who they treat like prisoners down in a basement; they get tortured. They cut you and put salt in the wound. If they do that, it never heals. I've also heard that some gangs brand people. If you want to join the gang you need to jump between two roofs and also to drink pee.

I don't intend to let anyone take me prisoner.

The warring factions meet at the basketball court at one end of Hörðaland. The teams set themselves up at either end of the court. There are no girl teams, but a few girls sit on the slope and watch eagerly. It's a great incentive to have the girls close by. It builds courage and resilience in your crew. You don't complain or howl in front of girls.

There're five on my team. There's me, Stebbi, Gummi, Alli Jens, and Kristján Þór. Kristján Þór actually lives on Hörðaland, but he has no friends there and since I'm his only friend, he's on our side.

Stebbi and Gummi have cool swords and shields. Gummi even has an iron helmet. I have my plank of wood, and Kristján Þór has a broken broomstick. Alli Jens doesn't have a sword. Instead, he has a length of rope with a knot at the end, a modern suburban version of an olden-day flail.

The other team has two more kids than us. I only know Bjöggi. He's my friend. Sometimes we play Action Man together. Bjöggi is a pussy and he's easily scared. I'm not concerned about him. But the others are pretty fearsome. I'm especially afraid of the two smirking brothers I recognize from school. They're famously crazy guys who always fight together. There's also a big kid on their team. He's two years older than the rest of us. I immediately pipe up.

- Big kids aren't allowed!

One of the brothers answers immediately.

- Kristján Þór is on your team.

That's right. Technically speaking, he should be on their team. He's also so tall that he is as big as the big kids.

They have similar weapons to us. Some have cool swords and shields but others have bits of wood. No one has an iron weapon.

The rules of the game are made by shouting them loud over the battlefield, to make sure everyone can hear.

- No hitting on the head!

- No throwing stones!

- No being CMO!

- No being CMO? Why not?

There's some discussion about this item. CMO is short for Count Me Out, which is when you take a timeout. What happens is that kids who are struggling in the battle shout Count Me Out! as soon as someone moves to kill them. That means they can rest for a bit and re-join the battle, refreshed, as if nothing has happened. Some kids do this over and over again so the game is both frustrating and unfair.

After some bickering, the warring camps accept that we're excluding Count Me Out entirely. If you get frightened, surrender. But that means you're out of the game and can't return.

When all the rules are agreed, battle can commence.

We start slowly. We each choose our opponent. I run straight at Björggi, hollering madly as I charge and preparing to hit him with all my might with my plank. As I expect, he falls instantly before my military might. He collapses to the ground before I can strike, holding his sword above his head.

- I give up, I give up! he shouts.

He goes and sits down. I look for another adversary. I see Kristján Þór fighting with the big kids and run over to him. Before I get there I get a whack in the back so hard that I get tears in my eyes. I turn around. One of the brothers is standing there, grinning his teeth and with a flat tree branch in his hands. My back smarts all over. He beat me really hard with the flat sword. According to the rules, you're not allowed to hit that hard, but since the girls are watching, you can't complain. I'm not going to make a scene.

We fence for a good while, parrying each other's swords, identifying strengths and weaknesses. He's strong and nimble. But he hurt me, so I'm allowed to hurt him. He knows it and proceeds cautiously. He won't stop grinning. I have to think fast.

Lightning quick, I strike at his fingers with my plank. He yelps and drops his sword. I raise my plank for another blow.

- Give up?

- What's wrong with you?

He's holding on to his fingers. I again make as if to thump him.

- Give up?

- You hit my fingers!

- Give up? I shout again.

He's about to lose. He should give up. I could simply hit him if I wanted. But I won't do it.

Suddenly the other brother comes up behind me and hits me on the arm with his sword; I drop mine. I run away and up the hill. He doesn't chase me, but tends to his brother. Then he picks up my sword. He looks at me. I look back. He takes both ends of my sword and breaks it across his knee. I gasp for breath, I'm so angry. That was out of order. These brothers are mental. I was just about to vanquish him. I could have hit him if I'd wanted.

I look across the battlefield.

Gummi is walking home. He's crying. Someone has broken his shield, probably the big boys. He's got a hardwood sword, made from the same material as the shaft of a sledgehammer. Stebbi is cautiously fencing with one of the boys, but Alli is running down the slope to stand on his own on the soccer pitch.

Kristján Þór comes running over to me.

- Are you all right?

- Yes, that asshole broke my sword. I got hit in the back.

- They're cuckoo, says Kristján Þór.

The brothers have got to their feet. They look angrily in my direction.

- Run away, I whisper.

I flee. Kristján Þór follows. We head at a sprint away from Hörðaland and up towards Bústaðavegur.

I have an idea. Across Bústaðavegur, where trucks are often parked, I remember seeing an old Christmas tree.

We hide ourselves behind a truck and peer around the side. No one is chasing us.

- Let's teach these nutters a lesson!

I make it to the Christmas tree and pull off some branches. Kristján Þór does the same. After a while we've got two large and fearsome branch clubs.

We lie in a bush and look over the battlefield.

Stebbi's gone. Alli Jens is still down on the soccer field. Of our enemies, just the big boys and the brothers are left. They're sitting on the hill and talking.

- Shall we go get them? asks Kristján Þór.

The anger seethes inside me. Those dickface brothers! Jerks who sneak up on someone and hit him and break his sword!

- Yes, I reply.

- One, two, and...

We jump up with loud screams and swing our clubs threateningly. The girls jump up and yell out. Then they start laughing.

The enemy don't know which way the wind's blowing. They spring to their feet. I run towards them swinging my club really hard in their direction. They flee, running into Hulduland and disappearing into a garden. We scream victory. We can occupy the hill. Alli Jens cheers and comes hurrying over.

We have to decide whether to give chase to the enemy. We don't follow them directly; instead, we go along another street and come from the other side of Hulduland. We crawl through the flowerbeds and gardens and sneak along the walls.

We're past the front lines, deep into enemy territory. Alli Jens is pissed, too. The big kid hit him and that's why he fled. He shows me where the sword hit his hand.

– He thrashed me!

– They're all insane, mutters Kristján Þór.

After some waiting and hanging around in the gardens, we finally see one of the brothers walking along. He's obviously coming from the convenience store in Grímsbær shopping center because he's got candy in a bag. In the other hand, he holds a sword.

We lie in wait behind a car. We jump on him and push him face down. Kristján Þór grabs the back of his neck and forces his face into the dirt. We take the treats. There are three bottles of Coke and three Liquorice shoelaces.

I lift his sword up off the ground. It's a carved sword with a tip. It's cool. He has spent a lot of time creating it. The hilt is a single piece, with a hole that passes through the handle. I take it and smack it against the sidewalk several times until it breaks apart. He doesn't say anything, but it's clear he's unhappy. He almost starts to cry.

I feel a little bad. That wasn't nice. It's bad to spoil the sword. But I still feel my back and there was no need to hit me so hard—or to find it funny, on top of everything else. He could have just surrendered.

And I think of Gummi. His shield is useless. Gummi started crying. His father made that shield for him. Anger flares up in me again and extinguishes any remorse right away. He deserves this.

We tie his hands behind his back with the plastic bag. Then we take the treats and run away.

We run away from Hulduland, the same way we came, onto Geitland. We go into the Grímsbær playground and sit there in the house, catching our breath and drinking the spoils. It's been one of the most daring street fights in living memory.

- He began to cry, did you see? asks Alli.

- Yes. Loser.

- You completely shattered his sword.

- I did.

- We should have held him down and peed on him.

We laugh. Kristján Þór is quiet.

- They're crazy. They'll come and beat us up, he mumbles.

He's afraid. I understand that. I know Kristján Þór better than anyone else. We have done so much together. We're best friends. We've stayed over at each other's. We've never really had an argument. It's not possible to argue with Kristján Þór because if he gets angry then he just shuts up even more than usual.

Kristján Þór lives with his mother and older sister. His sister is called Gréta. She's a teenager. It's really fun to tease her. She's always having boys over and cuddling with them and listening to ABBA.

Kristján Þór's dad and mom are divorced. His home is great fun. It's so different than my home. There's candles and incense.

In the hallway there's a book called *The Joy of Sex*. It's about people who are always fucking. The book has illustrations of all kinds of sex positions. It's the funniest book I've ever seen. We look at the book a lot when we're alone at his house.

Kristján Þór is no loser and he's not stupid. He's just odd. He's tall and has these large cheekbones. Some people think he's a bit retarded because he doesn't talk much.

Kristján Þór does everything with me.

Once, we made ourselves powerful rubber band guns out of the handles of paint cans, and by wrapping thick slings together from rubber bands we scrounged off the newspaper delivery man. That's thick, stretchy elastic. The guns were so powerful that you could shoot farther than you could see. Those were real guns.

Some teenagers who lived in the neighborhood close to Kristján Þór were always tormenting us when we were outside playing. These boys were complete idiots and would never leave anyone alone. They were in the Grímsbær gang. They teased us every time we went to the shops in Grímsbær; we were totally fed up with them. One evening we saw them loitering outside the shops. All day we'd been playing at shooting targets on fences with our sling guns. We'd practiced a ton and had become first class marksmen.

It was evening and we were on our way home. It was pitch black. We could see the boys well in the shop's light; we hid ourselves behind the fence on Grímsbær playground where there aren't any lampposts. We took all the slings we had left, shot at the teenagers and aimed for their nads. Then we ran away.

They chased us. We ran as fast as we could but they ran faster than us. It was like they could fly.

I threw myself behind a small bush and they ran past me. Kristján Þór saw that but tried to run all the way home. They got him. I was right there and heard everything.

– Who was with you? they asked.

– No one.

He didn't blab; he took the blame. That made it even more my fault. It's usually me who has all the ideas. Kristján Þór just does what I do.

They punched him in the stomach and face. And in the end they kicked him in his balls so hard he puked. The next day, he had a black eye.

We never talked about it. When the boys were gone, he went straight to his house and I went to my home.

Later that evening, his mom called. I was in my room and I heard my mom talking to her. She was clearly angry. Mom said it wasn't my fault. But I still felt a bit guilty.

I hope I'll never be beaten like that. I hope no one has an excuse to punch me or kick me in the balls. I once got a soccer ball in my nads and it was about the worst pain I've ever felt. It was worse than toothache. It was worse than stepping on a nail stick. The pain goes up through your stomach and into your chest, all the way up to your head—then it fills your entire body.

Hopefully the brothers aren't gathering a team of big, crazy kids. Some of them have motorcycles and they wouldn't take long to find us as we head home. Now I wish I hadn't broken the sword. Now I regret stealing the treats.

– I'm going home, says Kristján Þór suddenly.

He stands up and leaves. Alli and I sit alone in the cabin. We have a long way ahead of us, all the way from Grímsbær to home.

We don't go straight home. We decide to go down to the valley bottom and walk the lower streets and head behind Fossvogs School.

The trip takes a long time. We sneak like two frightened mice, running between parks and peering all about. At the least sound, we scurry for shelter. Our hearts jump in our chests. I still have the club to hand as a support. And then I really need to take a crap.

– I need to poop.

– Now?

– Yes.

There aren't any public toilets in the suburbs. When you're a long way from home, all you can do is knock on people's doors and ask to use their bathrooms. Most people let you.

I stop at a house and ring the bell. A young woman comes to the door.

– Can I poop in your place?

She looks at me for a while, searchingly. Alli stands back.

– Sure, go ahead.

I go to the bathroom and poop but come right back out. The woman is waiting for me.

– Thank you, I say.

– No problem, replies the woman, and closes the door.

We continue our journey. When we get to Fossvogs School we are reasonably certain that no one is looking for us. Alli is not at all scared. He really didn't do anything.

– Why don't we just go home?

– Yes, there's no one following us.

We crawl out of hiding. We're safe. We're local. We walk across the school grounds. Suddenly a cry:

– There they are!

The brothers come running. The blood in my veins freezes. I hear a motorcycle. Alli starts running and speeds up the hill. The boy on the motorcycle chases him. He's probably the bigger brother. I'm trying not to think about that. I throw away my weapon and run. I'm trying to run home.

– That's him!

They're after me. Because I broke the sword. If they catch me, I'm going to be beaten to pieces. I run harder. They're right on my heels. I hear the motorcycle approaching behind me.

I leap over the hedges by the row of townhouses. I look back. The other brother, the one who had the sword, chases me into the garden. The first two are nowhere in sight. They're not going to get me. They'll never get me!

I've reached my house. I'm home. They can't beat me up here. I spy a length of wood in the grass. Lightning quick, I bend down and grab it. I lift it up, stop, and turn around.

He stops, too. Looks at the length of wood I'm brandishing in the air. His brother and the big kid on the motorcycle are trying to find us. They shout but don't see us. Good for them. He answers them. He's not grinning. The dipstick broke my sword and hit me in the back sickeningly hard.

We stare each other down. I'm ready to throw the stick at him. Then it's like he realizes he's all alone and, moreover, a long way from home. I can see him hesitate. He looks behind and then back at me. He's afraid.

– You pisspants bastard shit, I mutter.

He was going to hurt me. He did hurt me. He thought it was fun. He has brothers. He has everything. He has a cool sword. His brother has a motorcycle. He's in the Grímsbær gang. They're going to beat me up. Maybe not now, but later. At school, or on the soccer pitch. There's two or three of them, and I'm just one. Someday when I'm walking somewhere, they'll show up. One of them will throw a ball at my head. They'll kick me in the balls. They're going to laugh if I cry.

He looks over his shoulder, then back at me. I throw the club.

It hits him on the forehead. He grabs his head. Then he takes his hand off and inspects it. It bleeds a waterfall. His palm is covered in blood. The blood spurts in rhythmical, slender jets from the wound in his

forehead. He's terrified. The expression on his face is one of despera-
tion. Then he starts bawling and looks helplessly around him.

Retard. Don't think you can hurt me! I'm not afraid of you. I'll
kill you if you come near me. I own you. I'm stronger than you.
I can kill you all.

I run toward the sound of the motorcycle. I leap through the bush
and head right for the boy on the bike. He's a teenager, definitely
five or six years older than me. He's unprepared. He's not wearing
a helmet. I strike him in the head as hard as I can, hitting him with
a clenched fist in the temple. He falls off the bike. The bike slams into
the sidewalk. It's still running. I scream. Someone comes running up
behind me and lifts me up.

- Have you gone berserk, child?!

I can no longer see. My eyes are full of tears. I hear only a buzzing
sound. I flail and kick in every direction and scream as loud as I can,
again and again.

- Motherfucker, motherfucker. I'll kill you, you motherfuckers!

The farmer has a wooden leg and walks with a stick. He's annoying.
So is his wife. They have two adult daughters, called Laufey and Erna.

Erna's all right. She often talks to me. She lends me books, too.
Otherwise, I'm not allowed to borrow books because I might damage
them. But Erna stole some for me: *Tarzan* and *Anna from Stóruborg*.
They're fascinating books.

Laufey's nothing but a grown-up. She hardly speaks to me.

This farm is different from the one I went to before. It's evil being
here. Everyone talks in an ugly way and says ugly things. They're
also always in a foul temper. I feel uncomfortable around them.

I'm scared of them.

All the same, I don't have to eat any more food than I want to. No one forces me to eat. That's good, because they eat tons of revolting things.

Once I came into the kitchen and peeked into the pot to see what was for dinner. I jumped back, startled. In the boiling water stood four teats. Boiled udders! That night, the farmer ate them.

As soon as I went to the countryside Grandma went into a nursing home. Soon after I arrived, I wrote her a letter:

Dear Grama I heard
You Went to a
nurseing home and
are in a bedroom
with a nice woman
I hoep she isn't
anoying it is fun in
the cohtree, there are
many sheeps ohe howd
and too cats, I'll see
You soon god bles You
my grama

✕

On the farm, there's a workman called Skúli. He's a man of few words. He leaves early in the morning to repair the fences and drive the tractor. Usually he's on his own, but sometimes I get to go along to help him. I like being with him. He doesn't say anything.

Once, I was ill. I told the farmer's wife.

- I don't listen to the devil's gossip. Nothing wrong with you but laziness. Get out of bed right now and go help Skúli outside.

I dare not do anything but obey. But I really was ill.

It was raining outside, and cold. I helped Skúli for a little while until I threw up. Skúli took me home and chewed out the woman. It's the only time I've heard him say something.

- This is more of your bloody folly, you old bat! Why send this wretched boy out when he's so sick?

- I thought he was simply being lazy.

- He's very ill; he's got a fever. He threw up while putting hooks in for the barbed wire.

- I didn't know.

- That's because you're so busy being bossy.

He went back out, slamming the door behind him. The woman looked at me.

- Crawl back into bed, you!

When I first got there, there was a young girl on the farm. She was handicapped in some way. She left soon. I think it was because she yelled a lot. Sometimes she screamed at night. I'd hear the farmer yell back.

- Stop your wretched howling, you imbecile!

When I had been on the farm for a few weeks I called Mom. I started crying when I talked to her.

- I don't want to be here, I whimpered.
- There, there. Don't be like that.
- Come fetch me.
- It can't be that bad.
- It is.
- Isn't there a dog on the farm? You can play with it.
- No, I want to come home.
- Be a good boy.

She wouldn't listen to me. I wept so hard that I could not speak for sobs and snot. The farmer's wife took the phone and reassured my mother that I was okay.

- You know, he's just a little keyed-up. He needs some fresh air.

A week later, I got a card from Mom. Inside she'd written: Darling son. It's good that you're enjoying the countryside.

I broke down and started crying. I'd never felt so alone in the world. No one cared about me and certainly not about how I was getting on.

△

I have to help out, here. I help with the housework and also stuff
outside. I get the cows and drive them into the field after milking. I
drive them from the hayfield, too. That's the most difficult thing to
do. The sheep run so fast and they hide in the ditches.

– Jón, there's a *skjátur* in the hayfield, the farmer says.

Skjátur are sheep. I go out and look across the hayfield behind the
farm. I don't see any sheep so I go back inside.

Everyone can see better than me.

– I don't see a sheep.

He lumbers to his feet, muttering curses.

– Damn, hellfire, Jesus.

I follow him across the farm.

– There, he says angrily, and points.

If I squint my eyes I can see better. I still don't see any sheep.

– Aren't there just cows? I ask.

– Don't talk to me about cows. Are you a moron, boy?

I don't see any sheep. I've no idea where to head. The hayfield is
massive. I stand, rooted to the spot, and wait. He hits me in the back
with a mighty blow.

– Are you being damn insolent?

– No.

– Get the hell on with it, then, you miserable idiot boy!

He lifts up his staff like he's going to beat me. I run away across the field. The grass is tall and wet.

Eventually, I see the sheep. There are two lambs. When they see me approach, they run away. They can run much faster than me. They hide, and I lose them again.

I stop and try to figure out where each of them has gone. It's like the earth has swallowed them. Perhaps they're lying down in a ditch or kneeling in the high grass. It's like they're invisible.

The devil-farmer is still standing on the side of the meadow. I'm so far away I cannot see him but I hear him screaming.

- Damn it, you bloody fool of a boy! Get the hell on with it! Get the hell after the sheep!

I run back to where I came from and try to spot them. I scurry back and forth, stopping occasionally to peer about. I see something and run towards it. It's nothing. Perhaps they've headed back the way they came.

- I think they've gone back! I call across the hayfield.

He doesn't answer. He's probably gone back inside. That means the sheep are definitely back where they're meant to be.

The tractor's driving along the lane beside the farm. Someone depresses the gas pedal hard, fast, and repeatedly. That heats the engine. It's probably Skúli, the laborer.

I watch the side of the tractor. Skúli must be coming to repair the fence so the sheep won't escape again.

I walk over to meet him. I like helping Skúli. We knock down poles, make fences, and fix them, too. I get to remove hooks with pliers and nails with a hammer.

I'm getting my feet soaking wet in the grass. But that's okay. It's not cold. I'll dry off in the sun.

The tractor draws near. I realize it's not Skúli. It's the farmer. He's pissed.

– You're a damned indolent idiot!

– They've gone. They went all by themselves, I say, trying to explain.

– Good-for-nothing! Do you want me to beat you, you devil-spawn? He drives towards me.

He swings his staff, and swings it in my direction. I hear it whine past my ear. I get scared. I start to cry. I hate this man. I'm afraid of him. He could hit me with his staff. I've seen him hit the dog in the hall. He waves the staff around him so that it swishes. I hate this shitty farm and everyone on it.

– Piss off, you worthless waste of space!

I run towards him and grab the staff. I smack him with the staff. The blow is clumsy and he blocks it with his hands.

– Go to hell, grave-dodger!

I hit the tractor until the staff cracks.

– Have you lost your wits, boy?

– Shut up, you creepy scumbag!

I throw the staff down and run down towards the farm. He comes driving after me. But he can't get out of the tractor without his staff.

Laufey's in the kitchen. She turns around when I arrive.

– What's happening?

I scream and jump on her and pull her hair. I pull her down by the hair. She cries out.

– I hate you! I scream.

She has a necklace. I rip it off her and throw it away. I want to ruin everything they love.

I jump to my feet, grab the crockery, and throw it to the floor so that it breaks. Broken glass shatters across the kitchen.

- What's going on? the old lady calls from the living room.

- Shut up, you disgusting crone!

I'm leaving. I run out. I'm going to go to the nearby town, Húsavík. From there, I'm going to get home.

I run across the hayfield. I'm blinded by tears. I get tangled up in the barbed wire fence and prick myself bloody. I don't care. I want to cut myself with a knife. I want to go deep inside and cut away whatever it is that makes me so bad far down inside. It's as if there is a cat inside me, scratching away from within. I hate everyone. I hate these people. I hate these sheep. I hate my parents for sending me here.

Skúli comes after me in the Land Rover. There's nowhere to go. I'm exhausted, too. My chest burns. I can barely breathe. I'm expecting someone to come. I'm going to go somewhere and never come back. If he tries to grab me, I'll bite him. But he doesn't try to grab me. He stops the car and rolls down the window.

- Come on, buddy.

His voice is calm. He isn't angry.

- I want go to home, I stammer out between sobs.

- Yes, I can see that. But why don't you first come and pull yourself together?

I sit in the car. I don't know what else to do. I don't know which direction to head. I can't find my way. Skúli doesn't speak; he just drives off.

They are all out in the farmyard. I sit inside the car. Skúli talks to them.

- What was that all about?

- He started raving all of a sudden, says the farmer.

– He came into the kitchen and attacked Laufey and broke and smashed things, adds his wife.

– He's not right in the head.

– And I'm guessing you didn't say anything to provoke him, says Skúli.

It's all stuck, inside my head. I don't remember what happened. I don't know what to do. I wish I were in my room. I'm cold. Even though it's sunny outside. I want to take a bath and sleep. I want to lie on the ground and be left alone, or go inside the giant thumb, further, further down, in through the heart and out the other side.

They take me into the barn. I cannot enter the house until I've calmed down. The old woman locks the door.

– You sit here and think about what you've done.

There are windows in the barn far up in the rafters. I take all the rakes I can find and break them. I take the shafts and heads and throw them at the windowpanes. They shatter. When I'm done, I lie in the hay and cry until I fall asleep.

Nobody says anything. Life goes on as usual. They've reached the conclusion that I am a useless, lazy, good-for-nothing. They leave me in peace. I don't know if they've called Mom. I don't care; she wouldn't do anything anyway.

No one cares about me.

After that, I always keep my pocket full of stones I've found in the farmyard. I choose round, heavy stones. I've declared war on the sheep. I hate them. Why are they always sneaking into the field? If I see them there, I try to stone them with rocks. I try to scare them from coming into the field. I don't hesitate to stone the lambs if I get close enough. That will teach those bastard ewes to play about in the hayfield.

Once, I found one that was trying to get through the fence. She was shit-scared when she saw me. I managed to kick her in the stomach as she was trampling away. I felt good about that. Now she thinks twice before she tries to sneak back into my hayfield. If she does, I'll kill her and cut off her head and set it on a pole so the others can see it, and the sheep will be afraid.

I've also got a stick like Hjalti has in *Anna from Stóruborg*. It's a rake shaft. I use it to jump over things just like Hjalti did. I get quickly around; what's more, I can even jump over ditches. Sometimes when I'm chasing sheep, I beat them with the stick.

Fucking ewes. They're stupid and disgusting and dirty. I hate them more than anything else in the world.

I hate the people on the farm, except Erna. But she's still one of them. They're all horrible. I hate my mom and dad too. I hate them for not caring about me. But most of all I hate the sheep. They're always mocking me. This is all their fault. They sneak onto the farm and hide from me, making me run all over the place. They absolutely know what they are doing.

I smack the cows with a whip. If they're being difficult, won't come from or go to their stall, they get a warning: I give them a sharp tap. If they don't listen, I smack them three times hard. I make them run when I drive them in the morning. They must obey me and do as I say. Otherwise, I'll beat them.

Snow White is my favorite cow. She is the most intelligent of them. She is always good and never fusses. Sometimes I beat her with the whip for no reason, just because she's there. I don't know why. Maybe I'm just evil. I want to hurt her. I want her to feel like I do.

Sometimes I feel bad that I've hurt Snow White so much. I sneak back into the barn and ask her to forgive me. And she always does. Sometimes I cry and hug her around her neck. And then she stands completely still. If she had hands, I'm sure she would hug me back. She knows how awful I feel inside. She understands what it feels like when I hit her with the whip. Snow White is my only friend.

I'm evil. Evil breeds inside me. I feel disgusting. My face is disgusting. My body is disgusting. I have ugly hands and I bite my nails. My voice is disgusting, too. I don't want to talk. I can't look at my face in the mirror. I try to avoid seeing it. When I brush my teeth, I look down at the floor. I hate myself. I hate everyone

✕

[…] Jón Gunnar is of reasonably normal size for his age, well-proportioned, but a little peculiar in appearance; his eyes rather deep-set, somewhat heterotropic, his coordination seems a bit awkward.

(National Hospital, Psychiatric Ward, Children's Hospital Trust, 02/04/1972)

△

[…] The boy has light red hair close cut on top, a freckled face and is stocky. It's sunny and a pleasant temperature on the days he comes here, but on every occasion he's always dressed up, wearing purple clothes and a coat—and he always has a cold.

(National Hospital, Psychiatric Ward, Children's Hospital Trust, 09/05/1972)

◼

[…] Jón is 5 years old, with red hair, close-cropped-an old-fashioned style. His eyes are large, light blue and somewhat dull. His eyelashes and eyebrows are white. He is well dressed, in his Sunday best.

(National Hospital, Psychiatric Ward, Children's Hospital Trust, 07/03/1973)

Later that summer, Mom and Dad come to visit. They were taking a trip and decided to stop by. It was in the middle of making hay. They camped behind the farm and stayed for two days. Dad helped with the haymaking.

They all liked Dad a lot. So much so, they were amazed such a fun and kind person could end up with such a terrible son.

When they left, they took me with them. Mom found the people odd.

I took my stuff and sat in the car. I didn't say goodbye to anyone.

When we got home, I looked at pictures Mom and Dad had taken that summer. There were pictures of them camping with other people. There was Kristín and her family and lots more people. There were pictures from fishing trips. Everybody was happy in the pictures. In one picture my dad was standing: in front of him lay so many fish. In one photo, he was smiling with some kids.

I don't know why I can't ever be brought anywhere. I don't know what's wrong with me. I find it frustrating. I would have preferred to be with them, fishing, than out in the country.

When I started school in the fall, my teacher sent me for a sight test. It turned out that I was near-sighted and had astigmatism and needed glasses.

My dad drove me to get some glasses.

I was taken aback, astonished, when we came out. The whole world had changed, shrinking in countless little details. Where previously there were fog-like blobs, colorful precision appeared. Until now, I'd looked at the world as though through water. My worldview changed in an instant. It was like I'd entered a new world, somewhere I'd never been. Someone had come along and changed everything. The light from the lampposts stopped being blurred and fuzzy. I found I could see forever. Esja was a mountain with slopes and snowdrifts instead of being a vague dark tussock in the distance. A hazy mist gave way to lines and contours on the trees and houses and garages. The light was amazing. I felt like I had been born again.

I recovered, and forgot all about the countryside. It was buried, hidden in the mists of the past, as if it had never existed. Until one day.

They were sitting in the living room and laughing when I entered. Mom was happy and was pouring them coffee.

- Who do you think came to visit?

They were totally different now. Even their faces had changed.

I didn't greet them. I didn't want to. I couldn't fathom why Mom had invited them inside. I went into my room and stayed there until they left. Then I went down and scolded Mom.

- What's wrong with you? I asked.

- Let it go.

- I hate those cretins!

- Don't talk that way.

- They're all total lunatics.

- No, no. They are not lunatics—they're just different.

I hate them, I said again. Mom shook her head and didn't answer me.

Had I done something wrong? Are others' actions always right? How are you meant to behave? What are these invisible rules that I don't know? What is "normal?" I don't know what I'm doing wrong.

I don't know. I don't know how to evaluate things. Am I an attention seeker, a selfish boy, an only child, a mistake? Am I good or evil? Why do I feel so much within my soul? While others' souls are seated on the very softest of plush couches, existing in a higher plane, it's like my soul wants to crucify me. While others sleep, I lie awake and chew my nails.

In the country, I was considered lazy because I didn't want to chase sheep. But I was not actually lazy. I like running. I just didn't see them. I didn't know where to run. I didn't see what everyone else saw. What they thought "normal" was a mystery to me. I don't see it until someone tells me.

Inside the car, I hide. I don't want anybody to see me in my nice clothes. They're silly and brown and made from a material that stings. I'm wearing a shirt and vest. My shoes are ugly, too: brown, creased smart shoes. Everyone will stare at me, like if they saw a monkey wearing nice clothes.

Mom laughs and teases me.

– Who do you think is going to see you?

I don't care. Preferably no one. I don't want to be in these stupid clothes. She made me to wear them. I don't want to go to this boring, silly theater. Plays are boring, except *The Pigeon Banquet*. And this is not *The Pigeon Banquet* but some boring adult play.

I lie on the floor in the back seat and stay there the whole way.

When we arrive at the theater, I slip into my seat and look straight ahead. I hope no one I know is here.

The lights go out and the play begins. And so begins the education of my soul: she soars from the muddy floor of the everyday and bathes in the magical light of the spiritual sun, absorbing every word and every gesture. What beauty!

The play is called *The Prodigy*, based on the book of the same name by Þórbergur Þórðarson. Þórbergur was a bit different. He was like me. He even had red hair. Maybe I'm not an idiot after all, but a prodigy? That would make sense.

I recognize this restless soul and my mind frolics back and forth across manifold existence—the soul's burning desire to seek things it can't know and elevate them above all things. I recognize, too, what it is to feel penetrating inadequacy and cultural limitations, to be always at odds with everything that seems natural and normal.

I'm lifted up out of my seat and swept up to the stage and embodied in and assimilated with Þórbergur. He's me!

I've found my soulmate, the lost link of my existence. Finally, after all my searching. Could it be that I'm adopted, after all? Somehow Þórbergur must be my father, if not biologically then at least intellectually. My soul is his soul. Is it possible my mother cheated?

Physically, I'm sitting stiffly in smart brown clothes, a twelve-year-old boy. But no one sees my soul dance up the walls in a crazy joy of newfound liberty. I'm in love. After this, I will never be the same person.

On the way home I forget to lie down on the floor.

■

Someday, it will be the year 2000. I don't know when exactly. I don't know what year it is now. I know I was born in January of the year 1967. That I know, but I don't know what it means. I've no idea how long ago it was.

When I grow up, I'm going to move to Arizona and become a real Indian and live just like real Indians do. I'm going to own a horse and live in a tent. I'm going to change my name. I hate my name. I'm not going to be called Jón Gunnar; instead, I'm going to take some cool Indian name like Big Eagle or Lightfoot.

I won't use a bow that shoots arrows, but a blowpipe that shoots poison darts. I saw just that on a television program about Indians in South America. After the episode, I went down to the basement. I found plastic pipes and made myself darts by winding paper together and making it narrower at one end. I put nails in that end and fixed them with clay.

My darts went incredibly far. Later, I made more darts and found wider pipes that could shoot bigger darts. I learned to make better-looking darts with sharper points. I stole large needles from Mom's sewing box and stuck them on the tips with tape and glue.

If I can't move to Arizona then I'm going to move to Þingvellir and live in a cave in the lava there and be an outlaw. I'm going to catch dinner in the lake and kill birds with my dart gun. I'm going to spy on people and steal what I need without them ever seeing me.

I'm not going to let anyone see me or know about my cave. I'm going to make my clothes out of reindeer skin. I'm going to stay awake when I want and sleep when I want and always have a blazing campfire in my cave. And I'll never go to town except to go to the library so I can borrow and return books that I'll read in the cave.

The raft is ready. I made it out of pallets that I fixed to oil barrels with ropes. I put a long stick in the middle as a mast. I stretched a sheet down it and tied it to the raft with ropes. I stole the sheet from my mother. Now, it has become a sail.

I write the raft's name on the side, using black paint from a can I found: KONTIKI, the same name as the raft Thor Heyerdahl sailed across the Pacific Ocean.

I'm not going to sail that far, just out to sea to fish for dinner. At most, I'll sail across Kollafjörður and over to Reykjavík. It's not that far. And maybe I can use the raft to sail between places and visit Runa and Grétar.

Runa and Grétar have recently moved up to Kjalarnes. They live in a small house near a bird farm at Móar. Their house was formerly the stables, but Grétar shovelled out the horse shit, replaced the windows and fixed everything that was faulty. Grétar works in Móar.

I can go and visit them as often as I want. I try to go as often as I can. If no one wants to drive me, I hitchhike. I stay with them all weekends and all holidays. It's better than being stuck in town.

I mostly play on the beach. I make lots of boats out of all kinds of rubbish and put them out to sea. I pretend they're under attack and I barrage them with rocks. If they sail away, they've escaped.

Sometimes I take hot dogs with me and grill them over a fire.

I can spend all day down at the beach. I gather stuff, light fires, and climb the rocks. At one point I tie a long rope to the fence stakes. Using it, I can swing from the cliff. Sometimes I go on a long exploratory expedition along the beach.

My raft is complete. It's good weather, perfect sailing weather. The fjord is mirror-still. I lug the raft into the sea. When it's deep enough in, I leap on board.

The raft is controlled by a single oar that I found on the beach, and a long punt. I'll use that to push the raft by levering it against the seabed or against rocks. The sail will come in handy, too.

It's hard to get away from the land. The raft is always carried back to the beach. I'm soon tired of pushing it out again and making sure it doesn't get stranded on any of the rocks.

A short way off, a little river runs to the sea. If I can get the raft there, I can use the stream from the river to carry me further out to sea.

I head back in to land. I use a rope to pull the raft towards the estuary. Then I leap on board.

This works better. In an instant I'm far away from the shore. It's gotten so deep I can't touch the bottom with the punt. There's not enough wind right now to fill the sail. Runa will certainly be surprised when I call her from Reykjavík:

- Hi.
- Hey, where are you?
- Oh, just at home.
- Home?
- Yes.
- At Mom and Dad's?
- Yes.

- How did you get there?

- I sailed.

Excitement shivers through me at the thought. It's brilliant, teasing Runa.

When she and Grétar first started living together, they rented the apartment in Mom and Dad's basement. Runa always came up during the day to get coffee and read the papers. She was pregnant and home a lot while Grétar worked.

Once, she'd made a salad in a bowl that was standing in the kitchen. I took some plastic bugs and put them on top of the salad. They looked really real. Then I went to school.

When I returned home from school, Runa had shut herself in the television room. She'd been there all day because she was so afraid of the bugs. She was so mad, I laughed. She was always teasing me like that when I was little. But if I had known she would be scared for real, I wouldn't have done it. It's very silly to be so afraid of bugs in a salad. What were they going to do to her?

After I've looked around and admired the view for a bit, I sit down and have my lunch. I have a Coke and a Mars bar with me. I lie down and relax. Sailing takes quite a while. Maybe at some point I can get an outboard motor to make the journey quicker.

Suddenly, I jump up from my daydreams because of a movement in the water right beside the boat. Sharks? I fear nothing in the world so much as sharks. I've seen *Jaws*. I've read books about sharks. They can attack boats.

I scan around me. A black shadow leaps forward just below the surface of the water. The hairs rise on my head. It was just one, but there are definitely more. I hope they aren't white sharks. They would easily shred the raft. Is this really the way my fate lies, being eaten alive in the middle of Kollafjörður?

I'm horrifyingly far from land. Kjalarnes has disappeared but Reykjavík doesn't appear to be visible. The sea is not so calm and gentle as before. There are waves, and the raft has begun to wobble ominously. The waves beat against the barrels and the sound reverberates within them. Maybe those aren't waves? Maybe the sharks have started to swim under the raft. I jump at each blow and look despairingly around the boat.

Suddenly the raft dips in one corner. I lose my legs and almost stumble overboard. Terror spasms through me. A barrel has come loose and is floating away. It was the only barrel not fastened with nails. I've never been so scared in all my life. Alone on a sinking raft surrounded by ruthless, bloodthirsty predator fish.

It's a horrible death, being eaten by sharks. I've read about it. You're swimming in the sea and see a shadow below you. And in my case it is even worse because I cannot even see the water. I'm so myopic, I can't even see a meter in front of me in a swimming pool, never mind a black sea. Sharks see quite clearly. They swim under the surface, measuring up their victim from a safe distance. The only thing you see is a black dorsal fin when it cleaves the surface of the water. Then it disappears suddenly and silently into the water and you don't know where it's gone. The shark swims below you and looks up at you as you wriggle helplessly.

The attack comes without warning, when you least expect it. The beast comes from the abyss with a gaping mouth, wide and black as hell and set with flights of sharp teeth. All of a sudden you're bitten in the leg. The shark shakes you and throws you back and forth so you don't know which way's up and which down. It stops as suddenly as it started, and vanishes back into the murk. It takes you a moment to recover from the attack, then you quickly realize you're swimming in your own blood. You feel your leg and find that there's a huge hole in your thigh, a gush of human blood. You can feel the heat from the blood seeping into the cold sea. You begin to lose your strength. Your vision blurs and flickers and you begin to swallow more of the sea. And just before you lose consciousness: the second attack.

God almighty! I grip my raft tight. My heart beats against the surface of the pallet with such force that the rhythmic taps sound on the empty oil barrels. Boom, boom, boom...

Such fear is uncontrollable, a mixture of vertigo, crippling anxiety, and psychosis. I would rather lie tied to a dental chair on top of Hallgríms Church with wasps hovering over my head and spiders crawling on my face than be here.

I pull my legs up towards me. Sharks can jump onto boats. There's cold sweat on my forehead and I can barely breathe. Far off I see the tower of Hallgríms Church in the distance. I've gone past it. I'm headed to the open ocean.

- God, don't let me die like this.

I clasp my hands and close my eyes.

- Dear Lord, if you rescue me now you won't regret it. I'll always do things really carefully from now on. I'll be kind to everyone I meet and never lie or steal or anything like that. And I'll never, never do this again. Amen.

I feel a little better after praying. I sit up and hold tight to my mast. The sail! The damned sail is carrying me out to sea.

I reach up high and tear it down. The raft is steady. I scan the sea around the raft.

Suddenly I hear splashing behind me. I scream and look back. Something disappears into the sea. Sharks! They've started to attack.

- Help! Help!

I scream in the direction of Reykjavík and over towards Kjalarnes and I wave my ripped sheet.

- Help!

Suddenly a face comes to the surface. It startles me so much that I fall on my butt. A seal. He looks at me, his searching eyes staring in disbelief. He's so close I can see his whiskers. He's not afraid of the sharks.

We stare at each other for a moment. I expect to see him tossed into the air at any given moment, sandwiched between the jaws of a great white shark. But nothing happens. Then he dives again. I see his shadow as he swims just below the surface. Or is that a shark?

I look very carefully around. I see, much to my relief, that there's a large rubber boat on its way towards me. The boat approaches at high speed; there's foam on the prow.

Rescue! It heads for me. Those damn sharks won't get this meal. Serves them right. I wipe away my tears and clamber to my feet. I'm not going to let anyone see that I was afraid of something.

I stand tall on the raft and smile happily to the police officers on the boat like a skipper with a clear conscience smiling to the agents at Border Control.

- Good morning, I say, cheerfully, once the rubber boat is flush against the side of the raft.

The policemen don't return my greeting.

- Get into the boat, says one.

I tumble into the rubber boat. I try to make out that I am perfectly happy and that all this is unnecessary officiousness.

- Where are you coming from?

- From Kjalarnes, I reply, proudly.

The police signals the driver and we head to Kjalarnes. Then he talks on the radio.

- Station?

Crackle and hiss. A woman answers.

- Yes?

- We've found the boy. He's fine.

Crackle and a little pause.

- Good. Where is he?

- Kjalarnes. We're taking him there.

Crackle and buzz.

- Take down his name for the report.

- Yes. Over and out.

He puts the radio back in his waistband.

- I saw a seal here earlier, I say, to say something.

They put me out on the beach at Móum where my voyage began. Before they say goodbye to me, they write down my name and address. Then they go.

The day after, there's news about me on the back page of the *Times*: "Alone on a Suicide Raft!"

I cut out the article. That's stupid, calling it a suicide raft. They'd never do that to Thor Heyerdahl. And his raft even got stranded on rocks and broke into pieces. My raft didn't break at all. Only one of its barrels came loose.

■

Mom recently bought a turntable for the living room. It's tall, with a plastic lid. It also has a radio and a tape recorder. It's called Crown.

Combined turntables are not as good as turntables that are on their own. Gummi has a Marantz. That's got a record player at the top and a cassette player and radio below. His turntable also has a diamond needle. The unit has an amplifier and something called an equalizer, which helps you manage the sound better. I can't hear any difference.

Mom and Dad don't own many albums. I've listened to them all. I like Þórbergur Þórðarson's albums the best. I enjoy hearing Þórbergur talk and tell stories about the south from when he was little. *Golden Slopes* is boring, though. Dad owns an album called *Buttercups*. That's very boring.

Buttercups is a long poem by Jóhannes úr Kötlum. Dad has all of his poetry books. I sometimes read them. "Star Steed" is my favorite poem.

Dad also has a book by Stein Steinarr. I think he's often entertaining. Some of his poems are very funny. I have to learn poetry at school. But those are extraordinarily long and boring poems from a book called *School Poetry*. It's an overview of all the poets. We only ever learn poems by men with muttonchops who are long dead.

Most of the poems are about something I don't understand. One begins like this: "Swollen was the air, heavy the sea, / spring thick and drowsy. / And Eggert Ólafsson it was / who pushed on past cold Skor."

I know the whole poem by heart. I had to learn it for school. All the same, I don't know anything about this Eggert.

I also know "Hiking" by Tómas Guðmundsson and can recite the whole thing faster than anyone else. I had to learn it last year. It's a good poem. It's about someone who is hiking and is very tired. I know what that feels like.

My favorite album is *50 Years of The Reykjavík Theater Company*. It's a recording of all kinds of plays. One called *God's Millpond* is quite good. There's also a play about Mount Eyvind. That one's pretty boring. My favorite play on the album is *The Pigeon Banquet* by Halldór Laxness. It's a funny play about an old couple who have so much money they throw it in the toilet. I can listen to it again and again and always laugh as much each time. I find it funny the way the actors speak. I've twice been to the theater for something other than children's plays. Kristján Þór and I went to a play by Dario Fo called *Can't Pay, Won't Pay*. That was good. And I went with my parents to see *The Prodigy*.

Mom says I'm similar to Þórbergur. I've been toying with the idea that maybe he's my dad. We're very alike, not only in appearance but also in the way we are. Þórbergur had red hair and glasses. After the play, I went straight to the library, borrowed *The Prodigy*, and read it. I also read *Hymn of the Flower*. I wasn't as impressed with that. It's really a girl's book. But The *Prodigy* is the best book I've read. Apart from that, I've not read many adult books. When I was in the countryside, I read *Anna from Stóruborg*. That was very funny. What's more, Mom once took me and showed me Paradise Cave. We couldn't climb up to it because it was really windy. But it was nice to see it. And I read *The Good Soldier Švejk*. Dad lent it to me. That was incredibly enjoyable.

Otherwise, I've only read books for children and young adults. I think I've read all the books in the library. I've even, I'll admit, read a whole bunch of girls' books just to have something to read. I think adventure books are amazing, especially about Indians. And I also enjoyed *The Hardy Boys Trio* and *Bob Morane*. My favorite book was still *The Windbag Bellows*. It's about a boy who's always pulling pranks, a bit like me. Now I mostly read young adult books: *Katamaran, Winter War,* others like those.

I don't listen to music much. There's no music at home, except a Christmas album by Mahalia Jackson, which no one enjoys. Sometimes I listen to a Sven Ingvars album that belonged to Anna Stínu. I enjoy some of the songs. I can understand the lyrics because I know Danish. I don't really understand English.

I inadvertently ruined the record player one time when I was playing Action Man.

My mom bought a big portable cassette player for the car. It has tons of good songs on it: "By the Rivers of Babylon" by Boney M, "Boat On the River" by Styx, and "Coward of the County" by Kenny Rogers. "Coward of the County" is Mom's favorite song. She sings it at home sometimes. When we go for a ride we play it and sing along together. I like doing that, but I'd never let anyone know. It's stupid. If I saw someone singing with his mother I'd make fun of him. Mom also has a sly fascination with Meatloaf. If he's on TV she always turns and looks at him.

– Look at how disgusting he is!

But she likes his music. She listens to the songs.

– He sings quite well, really. But he's revolting.

Dad has no interest in music. I've never seen him listen to any songs.

I've never heard him sing, except when he's just babbling something. All the same, he's in the police choir. I don't think that's fun. All choirs are boring except the Sunshine Choir.

My dad has even sung overseas with the police choir.

Dad thinks he sings well. Mom doesn't agree. She thinks the police choir is annoying.

Dad often boasts he has been abroad on a music tour. That makes Mom roll her eyes and shake her head. She hates it when Dad boasts.

- People even got up from their seats and clapped.

- Did they?

- We sang well.

- No, you didn't.

- Why do you say that?

- Because you sang badly. It was nothing special.

- Oh, it wasn't, wasn't it?

- No.

- Why not?

- It was more like screeching.

Dad gets mad when Mom belittles his choir.

- And what expertise allows you to talk like that?

- I just know the difference between singing and screaming.

- Why did people stand up and clap for us if we were that bad?

- Perhaps it was a courtesy? Or maybe they were glad you'd stopped screeching.

Dad gets pissed and starts listening to the radio. Mom sighs.

I'm getting ill. Mom says I'm *dommara*-like. Last night, I almost fell asleep in front of the TV.

When I watch TV I usually lie on my stomach in front of it. I watch with one eye at a time. When I get tired, I close that eye and look through the other. But yesterday, I had such a sore stomach that I couldn't lie on it. I was cold, too, so I lay down on the sofa with a blanket over me. I can't always see the TV when I lie there, but it didn't matter much—there wasn't anything interesting on.

I kept falling asleep and waking up; I dozed like that more or less all evening.

When the TV was turned off, it seemed like I was asleep. Dad picked me up and took me to bed. That was nice. He laid me in my bed and tucked me in.

- Good night, lad, he said quietly.

Sometimes, Dad is nice. He's quiet and talks to me and answers the questions I ask him without making things up. Those times, he bothers to play chess with me and read me poetry. Once he even took Gummi and me as outlaws up to Þingvellir. We camped and caught fish.

He's often tired when he comes home and I irritate him. His job is too difficult. Cops have to do so many things that other people won't do. I've heard my mother and her friends talk about it. He's always having to talk to drunk guys like Rubber Tarzan's dad and chase gangsters. Sometimes he also has to help people who have gotten into accidents and tell people about other people's deaths. Once, there was a man who threw himself from the top floor of the City Hospital. My mom knew about it because she was at work.

The police came to fetch the man. Mom saw my dad was one of the cops. I know because I heard her tell Aunt Salla.

Dad never talks to anyone about it. He just tries to forget.

Dad owns a ton of cop stuff. He has handcuffs and a baton and even a real handgun. He's the best handgun shot in the police and has lots of prizes. Once I got to go with him when he was competing. The men were all in a row, with headphones, and they shot at targets. Dad won.

One time when I was home alone, I stole his handcuffs and played with them. There's a strange sound when you click them together: klick, klick, klick. Then when you close them completely, they open again.

I handcuffed myself by mistake. I only meant to try to lock them and to slip my hands out of them but they fastened unexpectedly quickly so that I couldn't free myself. I had also inadvertently attached the other end to the radiator so I was completely stuck.

I was trapped inside my room for hours, until Mom came home. She had to call my dad and he came home from work with a key. They were still not that angry because I did it entirely by accident. Dad was just annoyed to have to come home from work. Mom thought it was funny that I had been there all day handcuffed to the radiator.

X

I leave my room. Mom is sitting inside the kitchen playing solitaire. She often does that when she isn't working or napping: she sits in the kitchen and smokes and drinks coffee and plays solitaire.

– Am I better?

– You don't have a fever.

– Can I go out, then?

– No.

– Why not?

– You know why.

– I'm done being sick.

– You need to stay inside for one day without a fever because otherwise you'll end up ill again.

There's no point arguing with Mom. Her word is law.

Mom and I don't talk to each other much. She does sometimes ask me how things are going and what the news is from my friends and what this or that person is up to. I tell her stories and she starts laughing. It's hard to tell Dad stories because he always stops listening in the middle of the narrative and goes off to do something else before I've finished, or else he interrupts and starts talking about something different.

Dad talks a lot about politics and what's in the news. He talks about it a lot when someone says stupid stuff. Dad gets angry if a reporter says a car has driven somewhere.

– The car drove itself? There was no one driving it?!

Mom doesn't care about that stuff. Dad often talks about the same thing over and over and asks questions you can't answer:

– Why did the man say that?

– I don't know.

– Is this normal?

– How on earth would I know, Kristinn?!

Sometimes Dad talks but Mom doesn't answer and keeps playing solitaire. Then he raises his voice more and more until Mom gets angry and shouts at him.

– Will you stop your bloody noise!

Then Dad gets sore and begins to watch the news on TV or listen to it on the radio. He feels unhappy that no one wants to talk about politics with him or tell him why people say certain things. Sometimes he just speaks to the television. During debate shows, Dad speaks more often than the people on the program. He asks questions and laughs at what the people say.

– What the hell is this dreck? Answer the question, man!

My dad is a collector. He collects stamps and all sorts of old stuff, buttons and stickers. He keeps a barrel out on the balcony full of pickled meat. The barrel mainly contains liver and blood pudding and sheep testicles, but also sheep bones and seal flippers and other things—I don't know what they are.

From time to time, some kind of "shipment" comes from out west for Dad. Then he gets very happy and puts it in the barrel. Often these shipments are packed in the newspapers that are wet and leaking.

I don't much like pickled meat. Often Dad eats it with porridge in the morning. The only thing I like is sour liver sausage. The other stuff I find disgusting, especially sheep testicles. I could never eat any animal's balls. Whale blubber and seal flippers are awful, too.

There's mold on top of the whey in the barrel. When it's hot outside, Dad sometimes skims off the mold and drinks the whey.

It can be interesting being around Dad. In the spring, he goes to gather the eggs of the great black-backed gull. I once got to go along. We headed out really early in the morning. We went all the way over to Grafarvogur and picked several pails of eggs.

Mom doesn't have hobbies, except for bridge. Instead, she brews alcohol. She makes rosé and beer. The alcohol is made in huge cans, which are stored in a closet. When it's ready, she puts it in a bottle. The rosé wine goes in large bottles and beer in smaller, brown ones. Mom even caps the beer bottles with a pressuriser.

Sometimes Mom and Dad's friends visit to play bridge. Mom gives them beer. When people play bridge, they put their cards down by striking the table with their hands. Dad beats his hand so hard on the table that I'm afraid he'll break his finger.

The whole family gathers from time to time for a bridge tournament. I think bridge is an annoying game. It's complicated. I know how to play Go Fish. Sometimes the three of us play Go Fish in the evening. My mom is amazingly good at cards. She remembers all the cards and always knows what to do next. Dad messes up a lot.

Mom and Dad are very different and have different interests. Mom's always alone. She's usually in the same mood: some varying degree of tired. Dad's more changeable. He can be amusing, mainly when he's doing something he finds enjoyable, but he tends to be distracted. I think that's okay. I find it worse when he's annoying. Then he nags Mom and scolds me. He goes on at Mom about her smoking or tries to get her to argue with him about something she or someone else said. I try to avoid him when he is in such moods, or else he holds me and makes me promise him something or other. And he complains about the fact that I've not done what I promised to do in the past. Usually, I don't remember what it was I promised. So I promise, just to get rid of him. He reminds me of Rubber Tarzan's dad, except he isn't drunk.

Sometimes he also asks me to tell him something. He takes my hand and holds me there.

- Tell me something.

What? I don't know what to tell him. I just clam up. He has absolutely no interest in anything I have to say.

I always say yes when he asks me to promise something. I daren't say no because then he just keeps me there longer and gets really mad. He always keeps me until I've promised something.

The promises can be pretty much whatever strike him. There are always challenges. Once he made me promise to write him an enjoyable story. But I was scared that whatever kind of story I wrote, he'd never find it good enough. It wouldn't be a proper story. I can't write; I write the dumbest stuff of everyone in my class.

■

SETTING:

An ordinary Icelandic home.
DAD *is sitting in the chair when* BOY *comes in. He is looking for something.*

DAD: *(friendly)* What do you need?
BOY: I'm looking for my sweater.

DAD *reaches out his hand, a signal for the boy to come to him. The boy comes over tentatively, and takes his outstretched hand.*

DAD: *(gently)* Did you do what you promised?
BOY: What?
DAD: Don't you remember?
BOY: No.
DAD: You were going to write me a story.
BOY: *(sheepish)* Ah...
DAD: Did you forget?
BOY: Ehhh, yes.
DAD: *(teasing)* Ehhhhhh?
BOY: *(sheepish)* Yes.
DAD: *(quietly)* Write a story for Dad.
BOY: Yes.
DAD: I'd like that very much.

BOY: Yes.

DAD: There's really nothing to it.

BOY: No.

DAD: *(quietly)* Will you promise?

BOY: Yes.

DAD: *(quietly)* A fun story for your dad?

BOY: Yes.

DAD *lets go of* BOY's *hand, offering him a handshake.*

DAD: *(loud and clear)* Agreed?

BOY: Yes.

They shake hands. DAD *smiles encouragingly and pinches the* BOY's *cheeks. We see the* BOY *go into his room. He sits on his bed, hides his face in his hands and weeps.*

THE END.

Mom finishes her game and lights a cigarette.

– Well now, shouldn't we get ourselves some dinner?

– What's to eat?

– I was thinking fried fish.

She breads and fries some haddock. I go into my room for a while.

Once the food is on the table, Dad comes home. He's in a good mood. He does a few dance steps with Mom. I start to laugh.

– Very flashy, says Mom and smiles.

– You didn't think I knew how to, did you? says Dad.

Then he kisses her and sits down at the table. He turns on the radio. The news clock sounds like a church bell. *Radio Reykjavík. Now, the news.*

We eat dinner under the roaring voice of the newscaster. We gulp down haddock with potatoes, fried onions, remoulade, inflation, invasion, weather.

Mom gives us yogurt for dessert. I lick the lid clean before eating from the pot.

"About 800 miles south-southwest of Reykjanes, pressure is settled at 988 milibars; off the west of Ireland, a growing pressure of about 986 millibars, headed northwest."

Mom and Dad are wonderful. I like being me. Perhaps we'll play Go Fish tonight.

"Improving weather conditions...excellent visibility...The hot springs...the weather conditions haven't altered...a little drizzle in the last hour...visibility fine...slight wave height..temperature: two degrees."

I got my first album, a Christmas present from Kristín. Packages from her are always labelled: *From Us in Norway*. The album's called *Grease*. You don't pronounce it *gree-arse* but *grees*. I don't understand why people write English totally different from how they say it. It's also been a movie. I went to see it with Kristján Þór. It stars John Travolta and Olivia Newton John. It's about teenagers at school: a new girl starts school and John Travolta falls for her. Everyone is dressed very strangely in the movie and they're always putting brilliantine in their hair. At first, I thought it was some new fad but Gummi explained that it was actually an old fashion that was coming back around. I don't know much fashion. I know about hippies. My sister Runa is a hippie. Hippies go about in smocks and clogs and sit on the floor rather than in chairs.

I really didn't enjoy the movie. People just start singing in the middle of conversations and then they all start dancing out of nowhere. But some kids I know have been to see the movie multiple times. There was an interview with one boy in the paper who'd seen it 80 times! What does his dad think about that? My dad would burst a blood vessel if I went to the movies that often. I tend to prefer action movies like *Wild Geese* or *Jaws*. I could watch *Jaws* over and over again. *Jaws* is an even weirder word than *Grease*. You can't say it: *Jafs*. *Joors*. *Jau-us*. At first, I thought it was pronounced *Javas* but Gummi told me it was more like *dwarfs*. I think English is complete bullcrap.

Why don't they just talk Icelandic?

I've been listening to some of the *Grease* album and looking at the pictures. The album cover has pictures from the movie. I think the best song is "Beauty School Dropout." I like to sing along to the chorus. That's the only bit I know. I lie on the floor with headphones over my ears. I don't know the words so I just hum and beat in time until the chorus. Then I join in with gusto and shout along, identifying completely, my melancholy song resounding around the house.

- Doobeeskoo-daba, Doodyskoo-daba!!

Tonight, there's a *Grease* Ball at the school. Everyone has to come in *Grease* clothes and we have to dance. You're allowed to bring a Coke and one candy bar. I'm bringing Coke but Kristján Þór is bringing Pepsi. He likes Pepsi better. I don't think there's a difference. Kristján Þór can't say Pepsi. He says *Fefsi*. We're both going to take a Mars bar. I've put a lot of preparation into this ball. I went to the pharmacy and bought a shiny black comb to keep in my back pocket. My mom bought me a tight black T-shirt. I wanted Wrangler or Lee Cooper Jeans but Mom says I have to use my own jeans. Duffy's, still. They're not as cool as the other brands. John Travolta wouldn't wear Duffy's. Also, I don't have a leather jacket. I'm going in only a T-shirt.

I went over to Gummi's to learn the *Grease* dance. Gummi is really good at dancing. He's nicknamed Gummi the Stud because once he went out to the convenience store and there was a man there from the paper who asked him what was the most fun thing to do at school.

- Play Kiss Chase with girls, Gummi said.

Sometimes we play Kiss Chase at recess. We try to get some girls and hold onto them and Gummi kisses them on the mouth. Sometimes the girls also chase us and try to kiss us. Most girls only want to kiss Gummi. Though Ásta once tried to kiss me.

The dance lesson went badly. I couldn't learn the steps. I could just about do a little something with my hands. In the end, we gave up. I think I'll dance as little as possible. Maybe just the last song, which is always a quiet song.

The main thing is the earrings. I went last week to The Thousand and One Nights variety store on Laugavegur and bought some earrings. I've not told anyone except Kristján Þór. There are several boys at school with earrings. Gummi has a piercing and a few different studs that he can put in on different days. I was going to get some Coke earrings. I think they're very cool. These tiny little Coke cans hang from a hook you fix in your ear. But they didn't have Coke ones so I got Pepsi earrings instead. I'm going to wear them in both ears. You're meant to go to a parlor and get them to make holes for you, but I can't afford it. I'm tired of talking about it with Dad so I'm just going to make the holes myself. I've managed to steal the big needle Mom uses to sew together haggis. I'm fairly certain that I can make a hole for earrings with it. I'll be the only kid with two earrings.

A girl at school has a crush on me. That's Ásta. She sends me notes in class and once even came to my house and banged on the windows. I haven't ever answered her. I'm too shy. I'm also afraid she might be teasing me. Perhaps she's just pretending to have a crush. I find it incredible that some girl could have a crush on me. I think I'm pretty ugly. I'm stupid, too. And if she really does have a crush on me, then she better stop now because I'd end up irritating her. Also, I'm afraid of girls. I don't understand them. They're like extraterrestrials. I never know what they think or what they're interested in. I don't talk to them. Some of them are unbelievably beautiful and when you look them in the eye you could go ahead and die. They smell good and when they speak, they have such lovely voices that you don't hear what they say because you're hardly able to stop yourself passing out. Then there are other girls who are pushy or just plain stupid and annoying.

Girls can often be annoying. They're also always saying annoying things. Perhaps that's because they're weak. They can't defend themselves and so they fight with their mouths.

I only know two girls. They both live on my street. I don't really know anything about the girls in my class.

Ásta is a typical girl. She's cute. She has long black hair and is quite small. I don't think she's exactly fun but at least she's not annoying. Though I find her girlfriends stupid and boring.

We meet up and get ready. I dress in my T-shirt and tuck it into my pants. We go into the bathroom to put on brilliantine.

I'm nothing like John Travolta. I've got red hair and freckles and glasses. I look more like one of the bad guys. In the movies, the bad guys are always uglier than the good guys. That's not true in real life. But I'm going to look a million times better when I've got my earrings in.

I smear brilliantine through my hair and comb it back. It rises forward again, as big as ever. Kristján Þór's hair always lies flat but mine has a lot of volume. I try to keep it down but it always springs up. In the end, I have to ask Mom. She puts hair spray in it and it finally settles down.

Outside, there's some frost. I get pretty cold as we head to school because I'm only wearing a T-shirt. I've got the earrings in my pocket along with the haggis needle. Kristján Þór is wearing his ski coat. It's cool. I usually wear a coat with a fur-lined hood. Some kids call those sort of coats Mong coats. You can't go to a *Grease* Ball in a Mong coat.

It's really important to dress right. If you're wearing the wrong thing, you're a dork. People judge you by how you're dressed. It doesn't matter when you're little but as you grow up, it's more important. No teenager wants to be a dork. So everyone wears Moon Boots and vests. I don't have Moon Boots but I do have vests and a splendid ski hat. I'm not a dork. I used to be, but not anymore.

I wasn't aware of fashion until we went on a school ski trip. I'd never been skiing before. It had suddenly become fashionable. Mom and Dad rented some skis from Sport Market for me. They were Rossignol skis. That's a cool brand. The coolest brands, though, are K2 and Salomon. The coolest shoes are made by Nordica.

I put on my skis. I tried to slide on them a few times outside the house and I could just about stand on them. But I needed ski clothes. My mom had some old ski pants. They didn't have any padding but they fit and were quite cosy. I only had a lamb's-wool hat so I borrowed a ski hat from Dad. It wasn't a real ski cap; it was all one color, fiery red, whereas ski caps are usually multicolored or have patterns. On the front it says, in large letters: NORWAY.

I met the bus up in the mountains at Bláfjöll. I hid the hat in my pocket because I wasn't sure if it was in fashion. But it was so cold up on Bláfjöll that I had to put it on. That's when I found out that it definitely wasn't in fashion. Everyone started to laugh and whisper to each other as soon as they saw me. They also made fun of my pants. All the kids had cool ski pants with padding. The girls immediately began to tease me.

- Are those jodhpurs?
- No, ski pants.
- Why are they so stupid?
- They're my Mom's.
- You're wearing your Mom's pants?
- Yeah, so?
- Isn't your Mom like a hundred years old or something?
- No.
- You wearing her bra, too?

Everyone started laughing. I was a dork. But I couldn't escape. The bus wouldn't return until the evening. I was forced to stay out all day in the pants and hat. I knew nothing about skiing. I went up in the chair lift but when I got to the top I got so scared I walked all the way down the slope on my skis and everyone looked at me as they passed, skiing.

I stayed inside the lodge the rest of the day and drank cocoa with Rubber Tarzan. He didn't even have ski stuff. He was just wearing the same clothes as always. And it was almost as bad to have his company as to be rejected by the others.

What a lousy day.

On the bus on the way home someone started calling me Jónsi Norway.

– Jónsi Norway?

– Shuttup.

– Are you wearing your Mom's panties?

I cursed Mom and Dad all day in my head. When I got home, I threw myself at Mom. I began to cry. I demanded cool clothes like everyone else. I'm no longer a dork. I want to be like everyone else. I want to be cool.

Everyone is dressed very cool. The boys are all in black T-shirts and jeans with turn-ups—even the complete dorks. Some are in black shirts and black jeans, like John Travolta. Some even have black leather jackets.

The only boy completely out of place is Rubber Tarzan. He's the biggest dork at school. He's tiny and has messy red hair he never combs. He hasn't dressed in anything from *Grease*. He's wearing a sweater and velvet pants. He's not even wearing sneakers, just black boots.

I feel sorry for him. His father is a loser and his mother is disabled and has to lie in bed all the time. He lives in Blesugróf. It's a poor area and those who live there are called lice-rats. One time, a few parents got together and gave his mother some used clothes their children had grown out of. But they didn't ask their kids first. And then Rubber Tarzan came to school in a new coat which one kid recognized as his own.

- Hey, that's my old coat! What are you doing in my coat?

- It's not your coat. It's mine.

- No way! It's got my name written inside.

Rubber Tarzan is poor. He smells bad, too. And he's annoying and stupid. Nobody wants his company. I sometimes played with him when I was younger because I had no one else to play with.

It was strange to go to his house. His home is ugly and dirty. Sometimes his dad was drunk in the middle of the day and would harangue us with some nonsense or other.

Rubber Tarzan also has a sister who is mentally ill. When we were at his home, she sometimes ran around buck naked and screamed really loud. It was really more awkward than funny.

Rubber Tarzan keeps trying to walk home from school with me. I don't want him to. I do my best to make it clear that I don't want to be his friend. I wish I'd never spoken to him. He's such a big dork that I can't afford to be seen with him.

He comes right up to me when he sees me and grins.

- Hi, he says, smiling happily and beaming his crooked teeth.

- Hi, I reply, indifferently.

- What's the name of the woman in *Grease*?

- Olivia Newton John?

- No, Olivia Nineteen Tons!

I smile awkwardly. This joke is months old. Rubber Tarzan is childish and still plays with Action Man. He stands with us. He's not going anywhere. It's unbearable. Kristján Þór is not really all that cool, either. Some kids think he's retarded. He also doesn't mind Rubber Tarzan. I wish that I was in any other group but this.

The girls are wearing short dresses and have curled their hair. Some are wearing tight black pants, red heels, and black shirts just like Olivia Newton John after she'd finished her transformation. I don't see Ásta anywhere. People are drifting in. The gym's still being decorated and they're playing songs from *Grease*. No one has started dancing yet.

I get rid of Rubber Tarzan and Kristján Þór and go into the bathroom to check my getup. My top has come untucked. I look more like Tintin than anyone from *Grease*. I silently curse my appearance. I wish I didn't have red hair. I wish I had black hair and didn't wear glasses.

I add more brilliantine to my hair. I look at the earrings. I'm not going to put them in before the dance starts. I'm going to wait for exactly the right moment.

I intentionally avoid Kristján Þór and Rubber Tarzan. Kristján Þór looks questioningly at me. I nod to him, friendly like we don't really know each other. He knows I'm brushing him off and he's pissed. That's annoying. But that's life. You can't be a dork forever. I don't have any other friends here but Kristján Þór, but I'd rather be alone than with him and Rubber Tarzan. They're standing alone in the corner, like they don't belong. They're still holding their carrier bags with the treats inside. I shudder to think that I was once like that. All they want for themselves is to pick their noses and play chase.

Ásta hasn't made an appearance. I daren't ask her annoying friends about her. Ingibjörg, one of the teachers, comes through the door.

– Alright kids, let's go into the hall!

The would-be greasers pack into the gym to the thumping sound of music:

You're the one that I want, you are the one I want, ooh ooh ooh, honey!

I roll with the crowd, making sure to keep away from Kristján Þór and Rubber Tarzan. I puff myself up and sing along with the song like a tough guy:

– *Jora voneravon!*

Or just: *Oh, oh, oh! Jora voneravon! Oh, oh, oh!*

Ásta has turned up. She's saying something to her friends. I watch them all look at me and laugh. It's impossible to know whether it's love or pure contempt. Still, at least she's not irritated with me. That's a relief.

The music stops.

- Everyone who wants to be in the group dance come up! shouts the teacher.

The developmental differences between the genders become howlingly clear. In just the past year, the girls have changed from giggling little girls into small, sedate women. They arrange themselves expectantly in a row. Opposite them, several boys mill about, looking around in the air, hands in pockets. Most of the guys are still sitting on the floor talking. Several have started playing with balls and climbing the bars, hanging from the ropes or even playing chase. The teachers shush them. I'm no longer a simple-minded child. I join one of the rows. The teacher claps her hands together and the dance begins.

Vellovellovellove! Tell mi mo, tell mi mo, diddi darada da! Tell mi mo, tell mi mo, didi dararada ra.

This game's unfair. The girls outnumber the boys—and they're taller. They also dance better.

I try to make out like I can follow along but I immediately lose the thread and get distracted. The song is too fast. I'm sweating and my eyes are smarting. When I wipe my forehead, I realize the brilliantine is starting to leak from my hair. My brow's all greasy. It's like someone has sprayed hair lacquer in my eyes. I excuse myself and head to the bathroom.

I dry the hair-lard off my face and wash my hands. It's like I've got whole slabs of margarine on my head. I comb my hair again. It's time. As of tonight, I'll stop being a dork who mucks about with toys and plays Fisheries by himself. I'm going to ask Ásta to be my girlfriend.

I take the earrings out of my pocket and put them on the counter. Next, I take out the needle. I tweak my left earlobe to numb it. I take the needle and I stab. First there's a little prick of resistance.

I push harder. I hear the skin tearing under pressure from the large needle. I breathe a sigh of relief and look at my ear. The needle has gone through the skin on one side. I keep going. There's a little stabbing sensation then the needle goes all the way through. I've got a hole in my ear!

I pull the needle out and pick up one of the earrings. I bend the hook and put it through the hole. It's going well but it's hard to find the hole on the other side. I've got these greasy fingers and brilliantine keeps leaking into my eyes. The hook is also made of soft iron which bends too easily inside my ear lobe. I may have to make the hole larger. I wipe my face and hands. I pull the hook back out and insert the needle. Now I can't find the hole on the other side of the needle tip, so I just stab a new hole. I'm beginning to bleed a bit. I still don't feel much. I wipe the lobe with toilet paper and make another attempt with the earring. Things go much better. The hook snaps through my ear. Now for the other one. I have to prick the right ear three times before I get the earring through.

I wipe up the blood and inspect myself in the mirror. I am more than magnificent. From either ear hangs a small Pepsi can. I try shaking my head. The cans dangle. Finally, I comb my hair and wash my eyes.

Myopics see very badly in the distance, but they see very well close up. We see things close to us even better than people with normal vision. I have a minus six in one eye and minus seven in the other. When I take off my glasses and focus in the mirror, I see how handsome I am without them. I decide to go back without wearing glasses. I wrap them in toilet paper and put them in my pocket.

I can't see properly when I come back into the gym. It's pretty dark. I can't see anyone well enough to recognize faces. I don't want to draw attention to myself; I try not to squint. I walk nonchalantly along the bars, feeling my way through the air with my hands. I'm hoping I'll come across Ásta. I try to fumble my way to where I last saw her. I hug the walls as I go, running my hand through my hair for reassurance. I feel the earrings, which are dangling loosely in my ears. I barely touch them. They hurt.

It's hot in the room and brilliantine is streaming down my face again. My eyes burn and I can't help weeping. This doesn't help my vision. I bury my face in my collar, rubbing away the revolting lard. Between the myopia, the tears, and the lard, I can't see a thing. The smarting's getting more intense. I can't bear it. I rub my eyes. I'm filthy with brilliantine. I've got to head back to the bathroom. I've got to rinse my eyes and clean myself up.

I can't see the door. I can't find my way back. I hear some kids laughing. I hope they aren't laughing at me. I hope no one can see me. I walk away.

Suddenly, the lights are turned on. I can see a little better. My eyes burn and smart. I reach into my pocket and get my glasses. I need to get to the bathroom. I hope Ásta can't see me.

- Oh my good God! What have you been doing?

I put my glasses on. Ingibjörg is standing in front of me. Her face wears an expression that's equal parts astonishment and worry. All around me, kids are standing silently and staring at me. I try to act manly.

- I was just stepping out.

She takes me firmly by the hand and leads me away. She orders the kids to remain inside the gym.

We go into the bathroom. The sight that greets me in the mirror isn't pretty. My neck and ears are covered in blood. My ear lobes have swollen to triple their normal size. My face is flooded with fat, sticky tears. My eyes are puffy and red and swollen. I rinse them in warm water.

– Is he okay? a girl asks. It's not Ásta.

– Yes, yes. Go back in, replies Ingibjörg.

I feel better. I dry my face and snort up through my nose. I daren't touch my ears. It's like the skin has been peeled off them. I'm bleeding from both lobes.

– What happened to your ears? asks Ingibjörg

– They're earrings.

– Who did this to you?

– I did it myself.

– With what?

I show her the haggis needle.

– Oh my God!

Ingibjörg drives me home. This sucks. It wasn't supposed to happen this way. I'm not cool. I'll never be a hotshot. I'm a moron. I always do everything wrong. I can't ever do anything right. I'm not like other guys. I've got red hair and I'm ridiculous. I can't play sports. I'm a half-wit who can't learn. Everything about me is ugly and disgusting. No girl will ever have a crush on me. Other kids have siblings and enjoyable home lives. Other families go traveling and do things together. We never do anything. And when Mom and Dad go somewhere, I can't come. For me, home is always majorly weird. My dad is a weirdo. He isn't like other dads. You couldn't even call him grandfatherly. If I try to talk to him, try to tell him something, he stops me and corrects me or mimics the way I talk. Okay, I do "ehhh" and "uhhhh" a lot when I'm saying something.

- Do you really need to say ehhh so often when you talk?

But I never say ehh or uhh so much as when I'm talking to my dad. If he can't work out what I'm saying, he moves on to something else, stops listening to me, focuses all of a sudden on my fingers.

- Are you still biting your nails?

I get distracted and look at my fingers. They're bitten down to the quick. Sometimes I bite them so much they bleed. I bite my nails, the skin around them, even my cuticles. Sometimes the wound festers. I don't know why I do that. I always have done. I've tried to stop but I can't. I immediately forget and start biting again. I do it unconsciously.

- Yes.

He takes me by the hand, hard.

- Didn't you promise me you'd stop with this?

I don't have anyone to talk to. Nobody tells me anything. No one cares about me. I'm like Rubber Tarzan. I'm all alone in the world.

◼

Jón Gunnar [...] has proved very stubborn and rebellious, so much so that his parents, who are quite elderly, have largely given up on raising their child [...] He often ends up in conflicts with other children, is on the one hand too controlling and the other hand afraid. His physical and his EEG were normal. Psychological tests and observations reveal that the boy is highly intelligent. He suffers from a considerable castration anxiety, he concocts some pretty extraordinary outlets for

his aggression, and he flees his anxieties most
uneasily. His sense of reality is good and his
ability for sympathetic insight is not in any way
compromised. In most aspects of his psyche, he's
developed naturally.

He finds that his environment has turned chaotic
but lacks the means and ability to change that.
There doesn't seem to be any doubt that the parents
have grown too elderly to cope with raising such
an unusually energetic boy. They have effectively
given up and the child has taken charge to a
pronounced degree, so much so that his security
is at risk.

Diagnosis: *maladaptio.*

(National Hospital, Psychiatric Ward,
Children's Hospital Trust, 09/06/1972)

It's like something's not right. Why can't I be like everyone else?
What's up with me? I'm no good at anything, not school, not sports,
not social activities. I don't even have good taste in music. What others
find easy and natural, I find complicated and alien. Everything I try
to do fails or breaks. And there's no one else to blame. There's something wrong with me but I do not know what it is. I'm abnormal.
I've nothing in common with anyone. I'm ugly, stupid, and annoying.
Maybe I've been cursed. Everyone else has normal hands. My hands
are always dirty, the nails bitten down past the tips. I'm embarrassed

that I bite my nails, but I cannot stop.

The future scares me. Everyone's headed somewhere together and I'm not invited. I'll go alone, somewhere else. I don't know where. I never know anything; I'm unable to do anything. No one cares about me at all. I'm all alone in the world.

I'm an Indian.

△

TRANSLATOR'S NOTE

I am translating *The Indian*, revisiting my childhood as the book's young narrator eagerly reads something his mother has bought for him—just the way I was as a kid. *Mér finnst gaman að Andrési*. My literal translation—what translators call a trot—would read *Me feels/finds good/fun in Andrew/Andrés*. Something like "I enjoy Andrew a lot."

I'm at a loss. "Andrési" is not an Icelandic name. And, several lines down, I find "Onkel Joakim" and the "Björnebanden." Uncle Joachim? The "Bear-band" or "Confederacy of bears?" The context tells me this is a child's comic strip, but my knowledge of 1970s Icelandic comics—limited, I confess—is being severely tested.

It takes an internet search to realize, via the Danish *Bjørne-banden*, that these last characters are the Beagle Boys, the hapless dog-like criminals I laughed at in the *Duck Tales* of my youth. Uncle Joachim? Scrooge McDuck. Andrés, or Andrés Önd, is not Andrew Duck, but Donald Duck, his name changed to preserve alliteration in translation.

Comics were when I first noticed translation, reading my way through Goscinny and Uderzo's *Astérix* series, about a small, unconquerable Gaul and his corpulent, near-invincible menhir-delivering sidekick, Obelix. And not to forget Obelix's indomitable terrier companion, Dogmatix! The dogmatic dog—a wonderful pun.

Yet in the original French, Dogmatix is not dogmatic, or not quite: he is Idéfix, a play on *idée fixe*, or single-minded. The potion-brewing druid called Getafix? Actually Panoramix, the character with the panoramic view, wise and all-seeing. In English, there's an added pun about finding one's next high—a pun that went over my head at the time, of course. The French reveals a second meaning to the English: to "get a fix" on something might be to get a read on it, to come to see it clearly.

What exists originally cannot remain, and yet there is a delight to knowing both the translation and the source. I winced a little having to turn poor Andrés back into Donald: he is, of course, Donald, but only after having been Andrés. To read Jón Gnarr in translation means to be unaware of Donald Duck's Danish-Icelandic detour. At best, there's a degree of surprise in an Icelandic child in the '70s reading a 1950s U.S. comic, but to American ears *Duck Tales* will sound expected. I find myself half-tempted to replace *Duck Tales* with a 1970s Icelandic comic instead. The situations aren't parallel, though: an American child reading an Icelandic comic would seem precocious. Besides, Icelandic comics didn't much exist in the 1970s; they've only really come into their own over the past 15 years.

The reason a translation can feel like a loss or a betrayal is that translation exists more purely *between* source and target language: where Andrés Önd meets Donald Duck and is perhaps both and neither character at once. I sometimes wish we could see the process of translation, not the product of it; even facing-page doesn't quite get that, leaving us with two texts to read, not the prolonged hesitation between them.

The Indian is a singular tale of growing up and finding you don't fit in. Yet, while there are universal experiences and ideas here—my version of setting fire to my bedroom was "washing" all my stuffed animals by flushing them around the toilet—none of us have *quite* these experiences, experiences which are Icelandic but not shared by all Icelanders, experiences which are shaped by the world beyond Iceland.

Indeed, the most difficult phrase of all to translate was the novel's final one: *Ég er indjáni*. I am Indian. I am an Indian. I am Native American. Transposed into American English, *Ég er indjáni* registers moments of colonization and cultural erasure. And, muted by the English, it is the wishful exuberance of a boy growing up on a cold, dark island, eating unspeakably horrific-smelling pickled cuisine, and wishing he were elsewhere, to escape, and so falling into some Hollywood-inflected romantic version of "the Indian." Falling into an impossibility, and not knowing it.

Perhaps, though, what the English brings to that sentence, the Icelandic already knows; the child Jón knows, the adult Jón, narrating, knows. I fight the temptation to insert a negative, hoping the reader can hear one anyway, in both languages. "I'm an Indian," I type. An Icelandic Indian, which means an American Indian, which means some *Lone Ranger*-esque version of the Native American.

What exactly that means lies somewhere between Jón's words and my reworking of them. This is an Icelandic story told in English: an American English estranged from itself by these atypical place-names and cultural references. No longer Icelandic, not quite English, and certainly not Indian. And that, after all, is what Gnarr's *The Indian* is ultimately about: being estranged, not fitting in: the boy who is told he is unruly, incompetent, and worthless, but who knows, despite everyone telling him otherwise, how much he has to offer.

Lytton Smith
Geneseo, NY

JÓN GNARR

Jón Gnarr was born in 1967 in Reykjavík with the traditional Icelandic name Jón Gunnar Kristinsson, which he legally changed in 2005 to reflect his mother's pronunciation of his name from his childhood and to drop his father's patronymic.

As a child, Gnarr was diagnosed with severe mental retardation due to dyslexia, learning difficulties, and ADHD. He nevertheless overcame his hardships and went on to become one of Iceland's most well-known actors and comedians. His acting work includes the movies *The Icelandic Dream* and *A Man Like Me* and the television series *The Night Shift*, which aired on BBC4. Gnarr published the first two volumes in his fictionalized autobiographical trilogy in 2006, *The Indian*, and 2009, *The Pirate* (the third volume, *The Outlaw* will be published in Iceland in fall 2015—DeepVellum will publish the trilogy in full in 2015-2016).

In 2009 in the wake of the global economic crisis that devastated Iceland's economy, Gnarr formed the joke Best Party with a number of friends with no background in politics. The Best Party, which was a satirical political party that parodied Icelandic politics and aimed to make the life of the citizens more fun, managed a plurality win in the 2010 municipal elections in Reykjavík, and Gnarr became Mayor of Reykjavík.

His term as mayor ended in June 2014 and he plans to use his post-mayor years to continue writing and speaking on issues that are most important to him: freedom of speech, human rights, protecting the environment, and achieving international peace.

Now that his term as mayor is complete, he has moved to Texas as Artist-in-Residence at Rice University's Center for Energy and

Environmental Research in the Human Sciences in Houston. Gnarr plans to focus on writing, speaking on issues of peace and equality, and performing stand-up comedy again, though he has not ruled out a future run for president of Iceland as his popularity in Iceland continues to grow after his successful stint as mayor of the country's largest city.

LYTTON SMITH

Lytton Smith (born 1982) is an Anglo-American poet and translator born in Galleywood, England. He later moved to New York City, where he became a founder of Blind Tiger Poetry, an organization dedicated to promoting contemporary poetry.

His most recent poetry collection is *The All-Purpose Magical Tent* (Nightboat Books, 2009), which was selected by Terrance Hayes for the Nightboat Books Poetry Prize in 2007, and was praised by Publishers Weekly in a starred review as "...fantastic and earthy, strange and inherited, classical and idiosyncratic, at once." He also has a previous chapbook, *Monster Theory,* selected by Kevin Young for the Poetry Society of America Chapbook Fellowship in 2008. Additionally, Smith's poetry has appeared in a number of prominent literary journals and magazines such as *The Atlantic, Bateau, Boston Review, Colorado Review, Denver Quarterly, Tin House,* and many others.

He has taught at Columbia University, Fordham University, and Plymouth University, and is currently a professor at SUNY-Oneonta. He has translated two other novels from Icelandic: *The Ambassador,* by Bragi Ólafsson (Open Letter 2010) and *A Child in Reindoor Woods* by Kristín Ómarsdóttir (Open Letter, 2012).

Thank you all for your support. We do this for you, and could not do it without you.

Dear readers,

Deep Vellum is a not-for-profit publishing house founded in 2013 with the threefold mission to publish international literature in English translation; to foster the art and craft of translation; and to build a more vibrant book culture in Dallas and beyond. We seek out works of literature that might otherwise never be published by larger publishing houses, works of lasting cultural value, and works that expand our understanding of what literature is and what it can do.

Operating as a nonprofit means that we rely on the generosity of donors, cultural organizations, and foundations to provide the basis of our operational budget. Deep Vellum has two donor levels, the LIGA DE ORO and the LIGA DEL SIGLO. Members at both levels provide generous donations that allow us to pursue an ambitious growth strategy to connect readers with the best works of literature and increase our understanding of the world. Members of the LIGA DE ORO and the LIGA DEL SIGLO receive customized benefits for their donations, including free books, invitations to special events, and named recognition in each book.

We also rely on subscriptions from readers like you to provide an invaluable ongoing investment in Deep Vellum that demonstrates a commitment to our editorial vision and mission. Subscribers are the bedrock of our support as we grow the readership for these amazing works of literature. The more subscribers we have, the more we can demonstrate to potential donors and bookstores alike the diverse support we receive and how we use it to grow our mission in ever-new, ever-innovative ways.

If you would like to get involved with Deep Vellum as a donor, subscriber, or volunteer, please contact us at deepvellum.org. We would love to hear from you.

Thank you all,

Will Evans, Publisher

LIGA DE ORO

($5,000+)

Anonymous (2)

LIGA DEL SIGLO

($1,000+)

Allred Capital Management

Ben Fountain

Judy Pollock

Loretta Siciliano

Lori Feathers

Mary Ann Thompson-Frenk & Joshua Frenk

Matthew Rittmayer

Meriwether Evans

Nick Storch

Stephen Bullock

DONORS

Alan Shockley	Cheryl Thompson	Michael Reklis
Amrit Dhir	Christie Tull	Mike Kaminsky
Anonymous	Ed Nawotka	Mokhtar Ramadan
Andrew Yorke	Greg McConeghy	Nikki Gibson
Bob & Katherine Penn	JJ Italiano	Richard Meyer
Brandon Childress	Kay Cattarulla	Suejean Kim
Brandon Kennedy	Linda Nell Evans	Susan Carp
Charles Dee Mitchell	Lissa Dunlay	Tim Perttula
Charley Mitcherson	Maynard Thomson	

SUBSCRIBERS

Adam Hetherington

Alan Shockley

Amanda Freitag

Angela Kennedy

Anonymous

Balthazar Simões

Barbara Graettinger

Ben Fountain

Ben Nichols

Betsy Morrison

Bill Fisher

Bjorn Beer

Bradford Pearson

Brandon Kennedy

Brina Palencia

Charles Dee
  Mitchell

Cheryl Thompson

Chris Sweet

Christie Tull

Clint Harbour

Daniel Hahn

Darius Frasure

David Bristow

David Hopkins

David Lowery

David Shook

Dennis Humphries

Don & Donna Goertz

Ed Nawotka

Elizabeth Caplice

Erin Baker

Fiona Schlachter

Frank Merlino

George Henson

Gino Palencia

Grace Kenney

Greg McConeghy

Horatiu Matei

Jacob Siefring

Jacob Silverman

Jacobo Luna

James Crates

Jamie Richards

Jane Owen

Jane Watson

Jeanne Milazzo

Jeff Whittington

Jeremy Hughes

Joe Milazzo

Joel Garza

John Harvell

Joshua Edwin

Julia Pashin

Justin Childress

Kaleigh Emerson

Katherine McGuire

Kimberly Alexander

Krista Nightengale

Laura Tamayo

Lauren Shekari

Linda Nell Evans

Lissa Dunlay

Lytton Smith

Mac Tull

Marcia Lynx Qualey

Margaret Terwey

Mark Larson

Martha Gifford

Mary Ann Thompson-Frenk
  & Joshua Frenk

Matthew Rowe

Meaghan Corwin

Michael Holtmann

Mike Kaminsky

Naomi Firestone-Teeter

Neal Chuang

Nick Oxford

Nikki Gibson

Patrick Brown

Peter McCambridge

Shelby Vincent

Scot Roberts

Steven Norton

Susan B. Reese

Tess Lewis

Tim Kindseth

Todd Mostrog

Tom Bowden

Tony Fleo

Wendy Walker

Weston Monroe

Will Morrison

ALSO AVAILABLE BY JÓN GNARR

Gnarr! How I Became the Mayor of a Large City in Iceland and Changed the World